Mulch Ado About Murder

By: Martha Rogers

ISBN-13: 978-1-946939-85-2
ISBN-10: 1-946939-85-4

Dedication:

To all my dear friends who have encouraged me
along this journey as a writer.

"This is the day which the Lord hath made; we will rejoice and be glad in it."
Psalm 118:24

Chapter 1

After securing Mitzi, my Schnauzer, in the bedroom with a few toys, I stepped onto the front porch of my cottage and locked the door. Not that anything ever happened around here, but one could never be too careful. Clear, bright skies without a cloud in the heavens filled me with energy. Nothing could go wrong on this beautiful early fall morning in northwest Arkansas. This was the day the Lord had made, a day to rejoice in the Lord's abundant blessings.

I stretched my muscles to remove the kinks, then set out across the way to the dining hall for breakfast, one of my favorite meals at the Spring Hills Manor Senior Living Community. I don't like cooking that early in the morning.

I gazed around at the fall blooms in the gardens and sniffed their fragrance, one of the reasons I'd chosen this place for retirement. Pete Simpson, one of the grounds keeping crew, rode a mower across the grass on the other side of the sidewalk. I waved at him and reminded myself I needed to ask him about bugs I'd seen on my rose bushes when he came over to mulch the azaleas at the side of my cottage.

Pete returned the wave before turning to head the other direction. I spotted several other workers trimming hedges and putting out new plants. One thing about this complex, they kept it looking more like a country club than a senior living center. At age seventy, I was just glad I still lived in my own cottage and not in the main building with the others who needed assistance with everyday activities like dressing and bathing.

I'd only gone a few feet when a voice called out from behind me. "Abby, Abby, wait up, and I'll walk with you."

I cringed at the hated nickname. Ben Martin, a retired lawyer who lived in the cottage two doors down from me, waved and hurried to catch up. That old codger insisted on calling me by the shortened version of my name. I much preferred Abigail. He also shared the same table at meals with me and four other residents. If I let him have his way, he'd be spending a lot more of his time with me. Not that I minded his company, but I wasn't interested in more than friendship.

He huffed and puffed when he reached my side. "You sure walk fast for someone our age. Don't you ever slow down?"

"And let old age catch up with me? Not on your life." I took great pride in my good health and mobility. No walkers or canes for me now or ever if I had anything to do with it.

I fought a smile. Not that it was any of my business, but Ben needed to get out and exercise more. He wasn't fat or anything, but he did have a slight paunch around the middle. Even with his six-foot height, he had a little more flab on his bones than muscle.

Of course I do have to admit Ben and I have fun teasing and taunting each other about politics, food, modern electronics, and anything else that happened along. I glanced back and found Ben a few strides behind. With a shrug, I strode across the walkway to the red brick main building.

Although the food here was relatively sugar-free, low sodium, and low fat, as long as it was cooked by someone else, I didn't mind.

I smiled at Lloyd, one of the attendants who opened the door for me. "Good morning. Looks like another beautiful day for us."

He grinned and held the door edge. "Yes, it is, and all but Doris are at your table."

"Thanks." I headed to the dining room in the East Wing of the first floor.

"Good morning, ladies, Harry." I settled into a chair across from Bessie Johnson and Harry Spencer. Clara Bivens sat next to me.

Bessie's beaming smile emphasized her Shirley Temple dimples. "Good morning, Abigail, Ben."

His silky tones floated in the air. "Ah, I may be old and too slow to keep up with Abby, but I'm never too old to enjoy the company of such lovely ladies." He slipped into the seat next to mine and winked at Bessie whose cheeks turned pink.

Why these women couldn't see through his smooth talk and gracious manner I'd never know. He must have been one smooth defense lawyer. But he could be just as ornery as any man I'd ever known, and that's what helped me keep my distance.

The remaining member of the table group, Doris Barton, arrived. After everyone greeted each other, Bessie and Clara warmed up to Ben and Harry. I gazed around the room to see the same thing happening all over the dining room where the women outnumbered the men at every table.

Some women never get over flirting and giggling like schoolgirls when men are around. I sure hoped I didn't act like that. But then I wasn't looking for another man like many of the females at Spring Hills.

The waiter brought a platter of egg substitute omelets along with turkey bacon still sizzling on the plate. Wheat toast accompanied by a low-fat spread and a bowl of fresh fruits rounded out the meal. I hid my smile at Ben's scowl when the young man served him a cup of decaf coffee. He wanted nothing but the fully-leaded stuff. He'd stop by my place later in the day to have some regular because I always kept a pot going. Then Harry offered thanks for the meal.

I unfolded my napkin and placed it in my lap before helping myself to eggs and bacon.

Bessie smiled at Ben and asked him if he planned to play bridge that afternoon.

Ben shook his head. "Don't think I can make it today."

Bessie cooed and flashed her dimples again. "But Ben, we really need to practice for the bridge tournament, and this is a good opportunity."

"I'm sorry, Bessie, but I already have plans. Maybe some other time."

I had to chuckle at his excuse. His plans probably included a long nap, but Bessie didn't need to know that. It also reminded me that Harry and I needed some practice as well since we'd signed up to be partners again this year.

Conversation continued to flow until Doris pushed back her chair. "If you'll excuse me, I'm going to change for my water aerobics class. See you at lunch, Abigail?"

I shook my head. "Not me today. I plan to have a little something at my place. I'll be back for dinner."

A few minutes later I left the others and headed back to my cottage.

Ben followed me outside. "Are you going to walk at a decent pace, or will I have to run to keep up with you?"

I didn't say anything but slowed my step. I kept in shape on the golf course every chance I had and joined the exercise class several days a week. Although I had invited him more than once, walking the eighteen holes of golf was not his idea of how to spend a few hours.

Ben gazed up at the trees dotting the area. "The leaves will be turning before you know it. There's already a chill in the air early in the mornings."

I nodded. "And it helps to have cooler afternoons for golf."

Ben pumped his fist in the air. "And football is the sport of the season. The Razorbacks are doing quite well."

"Yes, I noticed that." Everyone in Arkansas followed the Razorbacks whether they were affiliated with the university or not. Of course, with the center being so close to the campus, the Razorbacks became the topic of a lot of conversations around the table at meals.

When we arrived at the door to my cottage, I started to ask if he'd like a cup of coffee, but decided to let it go. I had a new mystery I wanted to finish by a woman who could scare the liver out of me, but I loved her books.

He waved and sauntered on towards his own cottage two doors down. My gaze swept across the manicured lawns of the Spring Hills Terrace center. Each of the individual cottages reflected the red brick and white trim of the main building. The brass trim of the light fixtures and door hardware sparkled in the bright morning sun.

Both Ben and I live in one-bedroom bungalows with a living room and a kitchen. I hoped I wouldn't live long enough to be relegated to one of the beds in the nursing section. Assisted-living might be bearable, but not the other.

Once inside, Mitzi's furious bark led me to the bedroom. She must have heard me come in, but she didn't usually bark like that. I let Mitzi out of the bedroom. She leaped up at me, almost knocking me down. She licked my face like I'd been gone for a week. "Hi, baby, you glad to see me? Let's go find a doggie treat." I gave her the treat and poured a cup of coffee.

Mitzi finished her treat, but returned to the bedroom where she once again started barking. I supposed she needed to go outside again. I grabbed her leash from its hook in the pantry, but before I got to the bedroom, she sprinted past me and raced to the back door, again with that furious bark.

A car door slammed outside and added to Mitzi's barking frenzy. I tried to calm her down as I secured the leash on her collar. Car tires squealed, and a motor roared. I rushed to the back door to see who could be driving like that, but whoever it was had disappeared. One of my neighbors must have been in a huge hurry to get somewhere. I shrugged and bent down for Mitzi who bumped her head against the door. "Okay, okay, we're going outside."

Each of our cottages had a small patch of grass and a patio behind it for a yard. Beyond that is a driveway where my white Camry still sat where it had been parked after a shopping trip on Saturday, so I didn't think any more about the car racing off.

Without any fences anywhere, I usually kept Mitzi on her leash, but after a few minutes, I decided to let her run a bit. After all, there was nothing around here to hurt her.

I sat in one of my plastic chairs under the patio cover to watch Mitzi, but she barked a couple of times and disappeared around the corner of the house. She must have seen or sensed a squirrel, but I didn't worry. She'd be back in a minute.

Mitzi once again barked and this time the frenzy clutched at my heart. Something was terribly wrong. She must have tangled herself in the bushes. I raced around to find her completely all right but furiously barking at something in the flower bed.

"Mitzi, hush, or you'll have all the neighbors running outside." I reached down to scoop her up and almost choked. Two legs clad in khaki work pants and work boots stuck out from under an azalea bush.

With trembling hands, I pushed back the leaves and found Pete Simpson lying in the mulch. Blood covered one side of his head and the ground around him.

The old adage, "scared spitless" came to me as that was the exact condition of my mouth. Pete lay face down in the dirt. He looked dead, and I hesitated to touch the body to find out for sure, but I placed two fingers on his neck. My hand yanked back in surprise. He was still very warm but very dead, and he'd been alive when I went up to breakfast an hour earlier.

My brain went into overdrive as I picked up Mitzi and hurried inside where I punched the call button for the medical personnel up at the center then dialed 911 for the Springhill city police.

A shiver raced down my spine, and I locked the door with Mitzi still yapping in my arms. Whoever did this to Pete might still be lurking about. Then I remembered the car leaving in a hurry. Had that been the killer? I called Ben and Harry. At this minute, I'd welcome them with open arms.

Now I knew what could go wrong on such a beautiful day.

Chapter 2

When they police arrived, I closed Mitzi up in my room and hurried back to the crime scene. Uniformed officers and plain clothes detectives swarmed like flies at a picnic across the lawns beside my cottage. The image of Pete, his own blood spilled about his head, wouldn't leave my head. His body lay like a limp doll under the azaleas. Yellow tape marked off the area, just like I'd seen on TV, but now it was in my own yard.

A rather tall detective moseyed to my side. "Good morning, I'm Detective Forester. The officers tell me you were the one who found the body and called 911."

"Yes, I am, or rather my dog found him."

"What is your name, and what time was that?"

"Abigail Billings and I had just returned from breakfast around nine. I let Mitzi out to play shortly after that, so I guess it was about ten after nine or so."

"Did you see anyone around?"

"No, I saw him when I was going up for breakfast. He was mowing the grass."

"Anything else you can tell me?"

At the moment I couldn't. He started to turn

away, but I tapped him on the arm. "Do you know the COD?" Proud of myself for knowing some of the jargon, I wasn't prepared for the frown that creased his jaws.

"COD? Just why do you need to know what killed him?"

I pulled myself up to my full height of five feet seven inches and peered at him. I couldn't peer down my nose as he stood at least six inches taller. "He was killed beside my house, I knew him, and I found him, or rather my dog found him." I planted my fists on my hips. "I think that gives me a right to know."

I waited while he shook his head and marched over to where the medical examiner or whomever examined the body. The detective hunched down, no mean feat for a man of his size. The one with SHCSU printed on his cap turned the body over, and my hand flew to my mouth. Blood not only covered the side of his head, but a garden tool also protruded from Pete's belly. No doubt about the COD now.

The officer glanced back in my direction. My eyes opened wide, and I stared slack jawed at the scene before me. He came back and spoke to me with a little more compassion than before.

"I guess you can see what killed him. The examiner says he's been dead less than an hour. It appears like he was working in the bed. Know why he was here?"

"Yes, I had asked him to check the mulch around my azaleas and to dig up some weeds I saw there the other day. Pete is on the grounds crew for

Spring Hills Terrace. I can't imagine why anyone would want to hurt such a nice man." I wanted to ask why so much blood matted the hair on the back of his head but decided the officer wouldn't tell me any more than what he had already.

Something made a tic-tic sound at a window. It was Mitzi tapping with her claws on the glass pane in a frantic attempt to get out. Oh dear, she didn't need to see all that blood and Pete's dead body. It'd scar her for life. I excused myself and rushed into the house to retrieve my darling. Even though she'd been the one to find the body in the first place, I didn't want her to keep looking. She had worked herself up under the blinds, so I raised them then picked her up.

"It's all right, Mitzi. I'm right here. Everything's okay." But it wasn't and wouldn't be until we found out who had murdered Pete and why. Through the window I spotted Bessie and Doris with Ben and Harry out in the crowd. The same detective who had questioned me now stood with them.

Before I returned to join my friends and share what I knew, I closed Mitzi up in the bathroom so she wouldn't be at my window again. At this point I didn't care if she tore my shower curtain to shreds. I just wanted her out of the way and safe. Her loud barking and scratching at the door followed me when I went outside. She really needed a doggie crate.

When I joined Ben and the others, they bombarded me with a gazillion questions as to how and when I'd found Pete and what had the police told me. I couldn't really answer all their questions, and I had a few of my own. Maybe Ben, Harry, and I could find a few answers. After all, Harry was a retired police lieutenant and Ben a criminal defense lawyer.

Bessie waved her hands in front of her. "Oh, my dear Abigail, what an awful thing to find in your flower bed. And poor Pete. Who would want to kill him?"

Even though the air was cool, she fanned her face with her fingers and gasped for breath. Better I had found him than her. She might have had a heart attack.

I wrapped an arm around her shoulders and glanced back at Ben. "There now, Bessie. Don't get yourself all worked up. We'll get to the bottom of this."

Bessie's lips quivered. "I'm going to be afraid to sleep at night with a murderer on the loose."

Ben stepped up. "No need to worry. Harry and I will take turns keeping watch for a few nights."

"Oh, that would be wonderful." She hooked her arm through Harry's and batted her eyelashes. "Having a former policeman on watch will ease my mind considerably."

Poor Doris said nothing, but simply stared at the spot where the coroner was placing Pete into a body bag.

After Ben and I solved the mystery of missing entertainment funds just last year, we were teased about our sleuthing skills. Ben liked digging for clues as evidenced by some the cases he'd won for his wrongly accused clients. Maybe we could solve this one and put our friends' minds to rest. I supposed the police wouldn't like that, but they didn't live here.

I whispered to Ben that I wanted to talk with him and nodded toward my house. We left Harry consoling Bessie and Doris. He gave us a searing look, but I just shrugged and grinned before heading indoors with Ben. Harry could join us later if he wanted.

Once inside, I offered Ben coffee. While it brewed, I rummaged in the drawer for my note pad and pencil. With both in hand, Ben and I sat down at the table while the tantalizing aroma filled the air.

"Sorry to take you away from the scene, but if Bessie knows what I am about to suggest, she'll blab it all over the complex."

"I take it your suggestion will be that we are going to investigate this on our own." Ben raked his fingers through his thick, white hair.

"Yes, that's exactly what I am doing."

"Well, we have ourselves a good mystery here. With so many people around this complex, it'll be hard to pinpoint suspects."

I resisted the urge to chew my pencil like I usually did when trying to solve a problem. "Let's look at what we do know, which isn't much. It had to have happened while we at breakfast." I slapped my hand to my forehead. "Of course, that's why Mitzi jumped all over me when I let her out of the room. She must have heard something and wanted to get outside." Maybe if I had taken her right away, we would have seen that car speeding away. It had to be connected.

"Hmm, too bad she can't tell us anything." He sniffed the air. "Is that fully-leaded I smell? The decaf they serve here doesn't help my thinker."

"You know I wouldn't have anything else for you even if it is supposed to be unhealthy." I filled the mugs and reached up to the cabinet for the creamer and sugar but stopped. My fingers touched the bag of chocolate cookies. If I were alone I'd indulge, but Ben would just have to get along with coffee. I placed the tray with the condiments on the table.

Ben reached for a mug and wrapped his hands around the warmth. He sniffed the brew with a satisfied grin. "Nothing like a good dose of caffeine to get my mind working. Now back to our murder victim."

"This will be a terrible blow to the residents here. Many of them will be too frightened to talk with police, and they won't feel safe until the killer is caught. Do you think it would help if we reassure them and ask our own questions?"

Ben drank a sip of coffee and nodded. He set his mug down and leaned back in his chair. "That's exactly what I think, Abby. Let's put our heads together and see where we go from here."

I lifted an eyebrow at his use of that nickname again. He shrugged his shoulders. "Abigail is too prim, proper and old-fashioned for the likes of you."

Well now, that put a different light on the subject. "I certainly don't want people to think I am prim and proper or old-fashioned. However, I like my name." Ben said nothing. I supposed that meant he'd call me what he wanted to.

Poised with my pencil over the pad, I asked. "Okay, what do we know? I saw Pete on the way to breakfast about a quarter to eight mowing the lawn between my place and the main building. That's quite a large area, so he must have been about done when I saw him. You joined me right after that."

"Right. You told the officers that he'd come here to work with your azaleas."

"Yes, and he was right outside my bedroom. I thought at first he'd just hit his head on something when I saw the blood on his hair, but then when they turned him over and I saw that . . . that . . . thing sticking out of his stomach I almost fainted."

Ben shook his head. "That *thing* is an aerator, and it served the murderer's purpose well."

A shudder shimmied down my back. I knew what the tool was used for. I'd used one enough times in my life, but for digging dirt, not stabbing. With those sharp points, it made a perfect weapon. I wrote on my pad again. *Fingerprints.*

"They're sure to find fingerprints on the tool, and then they'll solve this thing without us." Until that happened, we'd keep up our quest.

Ben furrowed his brow. "That won't work. The killer probably didn't stab him. Didn't you say he was face down?"

"Oh, yes, I did. He must have fallen on it after he was hit on the head. I guess either one could have killed him." I sighed. So much for that clue because now we didn't have anything to go on. "What do you think was used for the blow on his head?"

Ben shrugged his shoulders. "Maybe a rock or

another tool. Whatever it was, the killer must have taken it with him or her. Did you see his mower anywhere around?"

"No, but I figured he'd already stored it away." Then a thought crossed my mind. "Of course, it could have been on the other side of the walkway. That part hasn't been done yet."

I added *Check on mower* to my growing list. I stared at the writing a moment. "What would the mower have to do with his murder?"

"I don't know. Probably nothing, but we don't have anything else to go on, do we?'

I had to agree with that, but then I remembered the sound of a car leaving in a hurry. *Find out about car* went next as I explained what I had heard.

Ben tapped his fingers together. "You didn't see the car at all? Could it have been one of your neighbors?"

"I don't think so. None of us peel out of here like that car did. I wish I'd been quicker." I pondered the situation a minute. "Maybe we ought to check into Pete's background. Somebody from his past may have killed him." Then I slapped my forehead. "Ben, I forgot to tell the detective about the car."

"But you're not even sure it had anything to do with this."

"No, but . . . it doesn't matter. I can say something later."

"Hmm, maybe we could get Harry involved in finding out about Pete. He's an expert on the computer, and he still has ties down at the police station."

I didn't know what the computer could have to do with this, but I added it to my ever- growing list.

A clamoring sounded on my front porch. I shoved the pad into the drawer and hurried to check the noise. Then I recognized both Harry and Bessie's voices.

When I opened the door, the two of them stood on the other side in a heated argument. Bessie grabbed my arm. "Abigail, please tell this stuffed shirt of a retired policeman that no one around here is safe until this killer is caught."

Harry pushed his way past her, mumbling under his breath about crazy ideas of little old ladies. I grasped Bessie's hand. "Now, I don't really think we have to worry. The person who did this was most likely just after Pete and won't even bother us."

She pulled away from me. "Umph, you're as bad as he is. Can't you see the danger? And it was right under your bedroom window. I'd never sleep in that room again."

"And just where do you propose I should sleep?" I hoped she wouldn't suggest her house. I'd never find my way around all the clutter she keeps there.

She drew up her shoulders and with her full chest straining against the pink fabric of her dress, she reminded me of one of those pouter pigeons.

"I don't know. I'm just telling you what I wouldn't do. Go ahead and be brave, but don't come running to me for sympathy when something happens." She sniffed and toddled off to join Ben and Harry at the table.

Discussion about any type of investigation went on hold as long as Bessie sat with us. Soon as she left, we could tell Harry about the questions on our list.

"Harry, how long do you think they'll keep that yellow tape around my flower bed and that side yard? I can't let Mitzi out for a run until they're gone."

"I have no idea. It'll stay there until they're completely finished with sifting through every little clue they find. Might be a day or two."

That wasn't what I wanted to hear. As long as the tape marked the area, Mitzi would have to be on her leash. I refilled my mug and Ben's and offered one to Bessie and Harry. I decided to set out the bran muffins I'd made yesterday. I had to keep up appearances with the health food, but what I really craved was that bag of M&M's in the drawer. Oh, well, I'd pig out on them later then walk them off on the golf course.

"Here, these should go well with our coffee."

Bessie picked one up. "You and your health foods." But she took a big bite anyway. "Are you still going to Ellie's today and read to her?"

"Yes, after I play golf. That's when I usually go. No need to change her routine because of this incident. It would only upset her."

Bessie had that look in her eye again. Her brain was hatching up an idea even as we spoke. Sure enough she leaned forward in a conspiratorial manner.

"What if someone came in and was trying to rob your house and Pete saw him and ran him off.

Then what if that person came back today to shut up Pete, and what if he planned to come back and take more things from us?"

Ben's laughter exploded. "Bessie, that's the craziest thing I ever heard of."

Bessie pursed her lips and tilted her head to one side. "Well, you don't have to ridicule me. It could have happened. Things go on around here nobody else knows about."

My ears perked up. "What things?"

Bessie looked at me as if I'd asked for the key to Fort Knox. "Just things. I can't tell you everything."

Harry jumped in. "Well, I do agree we need to look outside the people here at Spring Hills. We'll let the police handle it." He patted Bessie's arm but winked at both Ben and me.

Ben rubbed his hands together. "Sounds like a plan to me. Let's get out of here and give Abby a little rest. This has been quite the morning for all of us."

Just before he left, Ben leaned over and whispered, "Harry and I'll be back after you see Ellie. We can talk more then. Meanwhile I'm going to do a little investigating on my own."

"Thanks, Ben. Maybe I should go check on Ellie after all the excitement dies down over there. Her windows face this part of the grounds, so she may have even seen something without realizing it. My first priority is to make sure she's not frightened and then question her."

"Good idea. I'll see you later this afternoon."

I stood on the porch for a few more minutes

after he left. Well, solving this little crime would take longer than the embezzlement solution had, but then time is what we had plenty of around here.

Chapter 3

With the police around questioning the residents, I had decided to wait and see Ellie after golf at my usual time. With the Razorback team as well as city officials using our course, tee times were precious, and I didn't intend to lose mine.

By the time I finished my game, the police were gone. As I approached the main building, the realization of the size of our complex hit me once again. The three-story main structure housed assisted living as well as independent living apartments. One section was set aside for those who needed full-time nursing care plus a new section is being built for Alzheimer patients.

With the number of rooms and employees needed to tend to them, we'd have a list of suspects longer than my arm if Pete was killed by someone who worked here.

I filed away that thought, so I could concentrate on seeing to Ellie.

Carrie Watkins sat at her desk near the entrance where outside guests registered. She was in charge of almost everything on this floor, and not much gets by her. "Hi, Carrie, I'm going down to visit with Miss Ellie."

The young woman's body jerked and her face turned ashen. "Oh, I wasn't expecting to see you. I was thinking about what happened to Pete and didn't hear you come up."

"Yes, that was dreadful, so I can understand your preoccupation."

Carrie gulped and ducked her head. "I must tell you, Ellie's a little agitated about Pete and all the police around here. I hope you can soothe her nerves."

"Thanks for telling me. I'll see what I can do."

Just before I knocked on Ellie's door, the one to the stairwell caught my eye. All the employees had access through that exit even though residents didn't. Any one of the staff could have gone out, killed Pete, and then been back in the building and on duty before he or she could be missed. I had to remember to mention that to Harry and Ben.

Ellie sat in her wheel chair, staring out the window. When I reached her side, I could see she had a clear view toward my house and all the commotion with the investigation. I cleared my throat, and Ellie turned startled blue eyes to me.

Her hand flew to her chest. "Oh, I'm so glad you're here. I watched the goings on out there earlier and was just sitting here thinking about it. Isn't it awful? Poor Pete, I really liked him. He was so friendly to everyone."

I kneeled next to her chair. "Tell me what you saw, Ellie." Could it be possible she had been an eyewitness?

"Oh, I haven't seen anything but those

policemen stomping all around your place. When I finished breakfast, I opened the blinds and saw them. I hope they haven't ruined your azaleas. I love to look out at them in the springtime."

I sighed. Of course it had been too good to be true. "I don't think they'll be harmed. After all, Mitzi does dig around in there sometimes." I gave her a hug then stood. "Now how about reading to you now instead of later this afternoon?"

I grabbed the book we'd been reading. "Here, we can pick up where we left off yesterday." I removed my glasses from my pocket and secured them behind my ears.

The pleasant atmosphere of the room with its view of the rose garden outside proved to be the perfect setting to read the inspirational romance novel, but my mind wouldn't stay put. I wanted to get back to Ben and the investigation. In the middle of a paragraph, Ellie leaned forward. I glanced up to see an impish smile play about her mouth.

"Tell me, Abigail. How are you and Ben getting along?"

"Uh, fine, I guess." Something was going on in that mind of hers, and I probably wouldn't like it.

Ellie's eyes sparkled. "You know what I mean. How are. . . um . . .things in the romance department?"

"Oh for mercy's sake." I tugged off my glasses. "Ellie, there's no romance. We're good friends . . . well, most of the time anyway." It sure didn't take much to get rumors flying around here.

"Humph. My eyesight isn't so good, but I can still see how he looks at you when you're teasing him."

"Oh, yeah, like he wants to do me in." I realized what I'd said. "Forget that." I placed a marker in the book. "We have a good time joshing each other, but that's all it is."

Ellie's voice took on a conspiratorial note. "You know, after that little mystery you solved about the missing money, everyone calls you the perfect sleuth team. He reminds me of that lawyer on TV . . . you know, Matlock."

"What?"

She grinned again. "Well, you have to admit he does look like him with his white hair and those seersucker suits he wears, as well as the fact that he's a lawyer."

I swallowed a chuckle and pictured Ben. Ellie did have a point. "I never thought about it, but he does. And I guess I'm Miss Marple, going around solving crimes."

Ellie shook her finger. "On, no, you're too young for her. You're more like that Jessica gal on that show about the writer."

"But I don't look anything like her." My hair was white, and I think I was taller than that actress.

Ellie leaned forward, her eyes with a more serious look in them. "No, but you love mysteries and solving them. And Pete's death is a horrible one. You and Ben could help the police solve it."

Wait until I tell Ben about this. On second thought, maybe I'd better not tell him. He might get the wrong idea. I certainly didn't want to get him thinking I might be interested in him.

I patted Ellie on the knee. "I think it's time for

you to have a little nap." She didn't protest, so I helped her onto the bed and arranged an afghan over her fragile frame.

"I'll be back tomorrow. We'll finish our story then."

Ellie just nodded, and by the time I reached the door, I heard her gentle snore. I told Carrie Ellie was sleeping and to check in on her a little later.

When I turned away from the desk, I bumped into Ben and almost jumped out of my skin. What was *he* doing here? "Good grief, Ben, you almost scared me out of my wits. You're supposed to meet me at my house with Harry."

"Sorry, but I was getting anxious. Didn't think it'd take this long to read to Ellie. We have things to do."

"Well, I know that, but you could have at least waited for me at the cottage."

He grasped my arm and led me to a chair in the reception area. "Come on, I have things to tell you."

I pulled my arm loose. I had things to tell him too, but if he was going to be so bossy, I just might not share with him and do this on my own. But then I realized I didn't have the resources Harry and Ben had, so I'd need their help whether I liked it or not.

He pulled a brochure from his pocket. "After lunch I went to see Mrs. Jensen. I told her I had a few friends interested in this place for retirement, so she gave me this."

When I raised my eyebrows, he added, "And that's the truth, Abby. I didn't lie. I do have two buddies who might want to live here."

I shook my head. Just what this place needed,

two more men like Ben. At least if they came, the other ladies would be happy. I turned my attention back to what he was saying.

"You know, if the person at the desk isn't watching closely, someone could easily get in and out of here in just a few minutes."

I peered at the blueprints on the brochure. "You're right." Then I shared my earlier discovery. After listening to my theory, Ben strode down the hall toward the exit. I waited for him near the desk. On his way back, he stopped in front of the linen closet and bent to look closer at it.

He motioned for me to join him. When I did, he pointed at the door.

"Looks like someone put some tape over the lock on that door so it would stay open. Who would do such a thing as that or why?"

"One of the attendants probably forgot his or her key, that's all. Let's go on back to my place to wait for Harry."

Someone gasped behind us. I swirled to find Maria, her eyes open wide. For a moment a flicker of fear darted in then out as fast.

"Please don't tell Carrie or Mrs. Jensen. I forgot my keys again."

I patted her arm. "We won't. At least you didn't lose them."

There was that flicker of fear again and she swallowed hard. "No, ma'am." She hugged a stack of towels to her chest and hurried down the hall.

Ben pursed his lips with his fingers and stared after her. He then glanced at me. "Now that was odd. I think we ought to stick around and snoop a little more."

As curious as I was, I was ready to leave. "I'm leaving." I strode through the exit into the crisp outdoors. Ben's footsteps pounded behind me.

"Wait up, Abby. Don't be angry. What about our meeting with Harry?"

"I don't know if he'll come or not." We never did set a definite time.

Ben stopped. "I can't keep up with you, so I'll see you at dinner."

I shrugged and waved my hand to dismiss him. If Harry stopped by, fine, but I had too much on my mind to digest for now. A raid on my stash of chocolate would clear my head and help me think. Right now I planned to return to question some of the other residents who lived on the courtyard side of the building. The police probably questioned them already, but they might say more to me. I also wanted to know why Maria appeared to be afraid, so I'd find her and ask her as well.

Chapter 4

After going over my notes and the events so far, I fortified myself with chocolate and a can of diet soda. After that, I hurried back to the main building so I could catch Maria before she went off duty at five. After seeing the look in her eyes earlier, I couldn't help but think something was wrong, and pure instinct told me it had something to do with Pete.

She stood at her locker in the staff lounge area preparing to leave. "Maria," I called, "I'm glad I found you. We need to talk."

When she turned to me, a look of pure terror filled her eyes. My instincts were right. "Child, I can see something is bothering you terribly. Maybe I can help."

Tears welled up in her eyes. "Oh, Mrs. Billings, I'm so scared."

Well, that was obvious without her saying it, but I put my arm around her shoulders and led her to a chair.

She pulled a tissue from her pocket and blotted her eyes. "It's about Pete."

Bingo! Maybe now I had a witness.

"Pete and I were dating. He'd been so kind to

me since my husband Jim was killed in Iraq last year."

Whoa. That bit of news came out of the blue and set me back a bit. "I'm so sorry. I had no idea about your husband."

Maria sniffled. "Not many do. That's why I came to work here. I needed extra money for our little girl, Grace. Then a few months ago Pete asked me out. He'd been so good to me and to little Grace. She loved him." The tears flowed again. "How am I going to tell her? Two deaths in such a short time."

Yes, that would be hard, but I didn't know what to say. "Oh, Maria, I'll pray for you both." I wrapped my arms around her shoulders, and she collapsed against me sobbing.

Then she sat back and dabbed her eyes. "Who could have done such a thing to him? Pete was the kindest man. He was always so willing to help people."

We sat quietly for a moment, but from the looks of her, something else bothered the young woman. She tore the tissue to shreds and kept her eyes cast downward. I reached over and lifted her chin with my fingers. "What else is there, Maria?"

She gulped. "Pete and I had an argument earlier this morning just before work. He wanted to give me money to help pay for some doctor bills for Grace. She's due to have surgery on her ears soon, but I told him I couldn't let him do that, and he got angry. Then I got angry, and we had a few words. Some of the others overheard us. I don't think most of them even knew we were dating until today, unless he told somebody. I'm not sure they heard what we argued about, but that's when I misplaced my keys. I was so upset I couldn't think straight."

"So, you didn't simply forget them." She was giving me a motive, and she had the opportunity, but I couldn't see Maria sticking a gardening tool into anyone's belly or smashing in their head, especially someone she liked. I could ask her if she knew of any enemies Pete might have, but several other staff members chose that moment to come in and get their things before going off duty.

Patting her hand, I stood. "We'll talk about this later." When I headed out of the room, she jumped up to follow me.

"Mrs. Billings, please, I didn't kill Pete."

"Don't worry, Maria. We'll find out who did this. You go on home and take care of your little girl."

"Thank you. I feel much better now that I've talked with you. I know God will see us through this. Pray He will give me the words I need to say to help Grace understand."

"Oh, I will. Of that you can be sure. God hasn't let me down in all my years, and He sure won't now."

She left through the employee's exit, and I headed for the dining room. Harry and Ben needed to hear this new information. We had to find out more about Pete and his background. Maybe that's what Harry could do on my computer after dinner.

When I reached the dining room, everyone was there except Bessie Compton.

"Sorry I'm late, but where's Bessie? She's usually the first one here." I unfolded my napkin.

Platters of grilled chicken breasts and bowls of fresh vegetables already sat on the table. Since the others had full plates, I bowed my head and said my own prayer before helping myself to fresh asparagus and a chicken breast.

Ben speared a piece of chicken. "Maybe she decided not to come in this evening."

Clara shook her head. "No, she would have called me."

At that moment Bessie appeared, out of breath and her face flushed. Harry jumped up and helped her to a chair. "Bessie, what in the world is the matter?"

She fanned her face. "I had the scare of my life." She paused for breath. "I took a little nap and slept longer than I meant to, so I was late in getting ready for dinner. When I turned from my mirror, I found someone staring through my window. I screamed, and he disappeared."

Clara's hand covered her mouth. "Oh my, I just knew something else would happen. No one around here is safe."

Poor Bessie, no wonder she looked so pale. Her house is one down from mine, but I couldn't imagine who'd be roaming around this time of day unless the police had returned. "Did you get a good look at him?"

"No. I called security, and I've been talking with them. It happened so fast. Soon as I saw him, I closed my eyes and screamed."

Clara shook her head. "I don't blame you, dear. I'd have screamed to high heaven myself."

Ben leaned forward. "Are you sure it wasn't

one of the groundskeepers or maybe a policeman still patrolling the area?"

Bessie bit her lip. "I don't know. Security asked me the same thing. They're checking it out." She patted her chest. "My heart is still racing."

I didn't think it could have been a policeman or he would've stepped forward and identified himself and apologized. I decided it didn't have anything to do with Pete's murder because it most likely had been one of the other men working around the grounds. Then again, it could be important, so I tucked the information back in my memory for consideration later.

Bessie needed reassurance. "It'll be okay, but let's have a little prayer right now." We bowed our heads, and I prayed, "Dear Lord, thank You for watching over Bessie. Please calm her fears and give her peace of mind. Amen."

"Thank you, dear. I believe I do feel better now." Bessie reached for the plate of chicken. "And I'm a bit hungry too."

I raised an eyebrow in Ben's direction, and he shrugged. We'd add this to our list of things to investigate later.

"I don't think you need to worry. With all the people around, I don't believe the murderer would return to the scene." However, that had happened a few times in shows on TV.

Bessie pressed her lips together then said, "If you say so, but I'll just worry about being murdered in my bed."

I shook my head. Bessie's imagination could certainly run wild. A few minutes later she leaned toward Ben and turned on that smile, her dimples flashing. "Don't forget we have another bridge tournament coming up, and we do need to practice."

Ben grinned. "We don't need much, seeing as how we're the two best players in the complex."

"Say what?" I sat up straighter and drew back my shoulders. "That's your opinion. Harry and I intend to give you a run for your money."

Ben raised his eyebrows. "Oh? I don't think so. Now as for the golf, I'll say you'll win the lady's division hands down."

"Thank you for that vote of confidence." I tilted my head to one side. "Seems to me I don't see you signed up for any of the events requiring physical endeavor."

His face actually reddened. "Well, uh, um, Abby you know I'd rather exercise my brain."

The others joined in the laughter, and Harry pointed a finger at Ben. "You, my friend, need to get out in the fresh air and get the kinks out of that overgrown body of yours. At least I enjoy a set of tennis now and then."

I had to stifle a giggle as I peered over at Ben. He sat up taller. "Humph. I can hold my own with anyone."

Oh, boy, that was a laugh. "That reminds me. I'm signed up for a tee time tomorrow afternoon. I dare you to join me, unless you don't think you have a chance. Do you have clubs?"

Ben spewed his iced tea across his plate. He grabbed a napkin and dabbed his face. "I'm not sure I can do that. I may be busy."

I started to protest but decided it wasn't worth

the effort.

From then on conversation all but stopped while we concentrated on our meal. I'd have thought they'd be buzzing about Pete's murder, but not another word had been said about it since Bessie's statement.

Ben folded his napkin and pushed back his chair. He smiled and touched his forehead with his first two fingers in a mock salute. "If you'll excuse me, I have things to take care if."

Clara laid her napkin on the table. "I have to visit with the old folks and help out with the crafts."

Now that was a hoot, and I laughed out loud. "Old folks? And what are we?"

The petite little lady waved her hands. "You know what I mean. The ones with walkers, and wheelchairs who can't see or hear too good."

"Oh, those old folks." I patted her arm and stood. "I'll see you all tomorrow."

Harry followed me, and we caught up with Ben at the door. I stepped through to the outside ahead of them. "Boys, I have some interesting news for you."

"And so do I. We need to do a little computer research."

Ben nodded but kept on walking. "That sounds like a good idea." Then he stopped and looked at Harry. "What's your feeling about what happened to Bessie a while ago?"

Harry laughed. "I'm afraid I don't take her too seriously. She's always coming up with something strange. It was probably one of the groundskeepers. After all, the rose garden isn't far from her cottage."

"That's what I think, and for all our safety, I hope that's all it was." Ben resumed his stride. "How about a game of rummy or dominoes after we finish our research?"

Harry shook his head. "Not tonight. Besides, bridge is my game, remember?"

Ben shook his head and chuckled. "How could I forget? You and Abby almost beat us in the last tournament, but this time we'll be so far ahead, you'll never catch up."

"Don't count on it friend. Abigail is much sharper than Bessie."

Now that was an interesting comment coming from Harry. I liked to think I was smarter than Bessie at bridge, but didn't realize Harry might think so, too.

We reached my house and when I unlocked my door, Mitzi greeted us with her happy dance. "Hey, pretty baby, I'm glad to see you." I knew we couldn't get anything done with her around. She loved Ben and would be jumping all over him even though he didn't return the love. I put her in the bedroom and closed the door. She protested, but soon settled down with some of the toys I had left in the room. At least I *hoped* it was the toys that quieted her.

In just a few minutes a pot of coffee brewed on the counter. I retrieved a chocolate pie from the fridge. Harry and Ben would both enjoy a piece after our dessert of fruit and gelatin at dinner. They didn't need to know it had come from the grocery store.

When I set it on the counter, Harry rubbed his

hands together. "Man, this looks good enough to eat." He grinned. "I had no idea you kept that kind of stuff around."

I smiled and wondered what he'd think of the taco chips, bean dip, chocolate candy, and cookies in my pantry. Next to those, this little pie was nothing. I served them a large slice and poured the coffee.

Harry picked up his fork. "This is just what I need to get my brain cells to working." He took a bite and breathed deeply. "Ah, perfect."

He was just like Ben and most men I'd known. Give them something good to eat, and they were happy.

Ben swallowed his bite and grinned with pleasure. Then he asked about my news.

I told them about Maria and Pete and their argument.

Ben pursed his lips. "Now that doesn't look good, but I can't see her doing anything to hurt Pete."

"My feelings exactly." I leaned on my forearms with my hands clasped. "Just what do we know about Pete Simpson?"

Harry tapped his fingers on the table. "That's what I meant about computer research."

I walked over to my computer and turned it on. In a few seconds my icons appeared, and I clicked on my server. Harry finished his pie then joined me.

"Okay, Mr. Police Officer, how do we find out about Pete other than Google his name? I have his address and not much else." I typed his name into the search box.

Harry tapped my shoulder. "Let me try. I have access to some things you wouldn't know about."

He sat down, and his fingers flew over the keys. For a man with such big fingers, his typing speed amazed me. Then I saw Pete Simpson's name come up on the screen.

"Well, now, looky here. Our Mr. Pete had his own blog."

I slipped on my glasses and read about Pete's gardening tips. I didn't see that had much to do with his murder.

Harry kept searching and came up with an arrest for DUI and disorderly conduct. I wasn't sure how Harry came up with this, and at the moment I didn't want to know. The idea you could find out so much about a person was a little too scary if you asked me.

Ben stood beside me, reading the words on the monitor. He whistled under his breath. "I'd say that puts a whole new light on things. Could he have some other stuff we don't know about yet?"

Harry made a few notes then clicked off the site. "I'll look into this further." He turned to me and skewed his mouth. "One of us needs to talk to some of the others on the grounds crew and see if they know anything about Pete. I'm going to see what the detectives found out because I'm sure they've questioned a bunch of people around here. We can do the same since employees as well as residents may be willing to tell us more than they told the law."

I had already decided to do that, so I volunteered for the job. After a few more searches turned up nothing new, we decided to take care of those things tomorrow.

After they left, I freed Mitzi from her prison and took her outside but kept her on the leash. While she did her business, I gazed across at the main building. All of the windows on Ellie's wing looked directly over at my house. In my haste this afternoon, I had forgotten to check that. Any one of these residents could have seen everything that happened. First thing in the morning I'd have to find out exactly who had rooms facing my cottage and start my questioning there.

Chapter 5

O n Thursday, after spending a restless night with visions of Pete lying in the mulch, ideas of who could be guilty rolled through my mind like tumbleweeds across the prairie in those old Western movies I liked to watch. I turned over and opened my eyes. The clock beamed its red numbers of 6:30 in my face. I pushed back the covers, waking Mitzi in the process. She yelped and jumped from the bed, not very happy that I had disturbed her sleep. No matter that she did that to me most mornings.

I shoved my feet into slippers and shrugged on a terry robe and tied the belt around my waist. Mitzi and I made our way out the back door. I'd be glad when I could let my baby have her morning run. As it was, she had to be on the leash until the crime scene people released my yard. Of course, Mitzi didn't like that a bit. She jumped and twisted in an effort to get loose.

After a few minutes we were back inside. I filled her bowl and let her eat while I poured my coffee and opened my Bible for some quiet time. Spending time with the Lord each morning helped clear me to my mind and prepare for the day.

After the prayer time, I made a list of what needed to be done and finished my coffee. First item was to get the names of the tenants on Ellie's wing and then interview them. Next, I would have to seek out the grounds crew and question them about Pete. Then I crossed that off. Harry could take care of that. On second thought, maybe I did need to talk to the man in charge. I wrote his name on my list.

I pulled on a fleece jacket for the brief walk to the main building. Not long and the mornings would be colder which meant many of those in the cottages would opt for breakfast in their own kitchens, but not me. I found the cold air invigorating.

Conversation buzzed in the dining hall, and I heard snatches with Pete's name. I reached our table and sat next to Doris. Although she participates in activities, she is almost always quiet and never says much to any of us outside of the dining room. I could tell something bothered her because she only picked at her food this morning. However, getting information from her was harder than getting past security at the airport.

Bessie, Harry, and Ben talked about nothing but the bridge tournament coming up, so I moved my chair closer to Doris. "Is there something troubling you this morning? You seem to be a little distraught."

She bit her lip. "I'm just upset about Pete."

"We all are. It's a tragic thing." But there had to be more to her distress than that since it had affected all of us.

Doris clasped her hands together and leaned toward me. "Can you come by and talk to me later? I don't want to say anything around the others."

"Of course I can. I have some errands to do this morning, but I'll stop by your house soon as I'm done." Surely Doris was just upset because a young man had died. I didn't think she could have any other information that would be useful, but I would certainly try to see her before lunch.

"I hate to leave such good company, but I need to get started on my errands. Have a great morning." I nodded to Ben and Harry. "I'll see you this afternoon."

I left them and headed for my first stop, the director's office. Noreen Jensen sat at her desk talking on the phone. I knocked lightly on the door frame and she beckoned me into her office. A moment later she ended her call.

"Abigail, have a seat. The executive board had a meeting this morning. That was Mr. Wentworth, the chairman on the phone. They are really upset over this . . . this murder. They know the publicity will get to some of our families, and we may be losing residents."

That was understandable of course, but it would take a while if they wanted to find other places as nice as this one. By then this whole matter would be cleared up and there would be no need for anyone moving. Then again, if Pete turned out to be mixed up in anything illegal, that might be just as bad. It would look like the manager didn't do a more careful job of screening employees.

Noreen blew out a breath and leaned back in

her chair. "How can I help you?"

I eased into the leather chair across from her. "In some ways it has to do with the death of Pete."

Then she sighed and leaned back. "I should have realized you would get involved. How can I help you?"

At least she didn't think I was meddling. "The rooms in the wing where Ellie Davenport lives have a clear view down to my house. Ellie didn't see anything because she didn't open her blinds until later, after the police had come. I thought maybe someone else might have seen something, maybe without even realizing it. Perhaps if I question them, they will tell me if they did."

Noreen stared at me a moment before whipping around to the computer behind her. "I see. I don't know what good it'll do, but I suppose you have Ben Martin helping you."

She had me with that one, but I was only doing it for the sake of all the people who live here. "Yes, I do, and Harry is helping as well. We promise we're not getting into the way of the police."

"They spoke to a few of our residents and will come back later to talk with others." Noreen clicked on a page and hit the printer icon. "But they're rather intimidating, so they most likely didn't get many clear answers. Also, the police have a tendency to dismiss much of what our older people have to say."

She had that right. Even so, I hoped they didn't think we were too old to be reliable witnesses. So many others don't understand that even those in their later years can be just as observant as someone much younger. If the detective didn't send anyone back right away, Ben and I could get the jump on them.

Noreen retrieved a sheet of paper from her printer. "Here you go. This is everyone on that wing. You can cross through the odd number rooms as they face the inner courtyard and not the outside."

"Thank you. I'll be discreet as I question them."

"On another topic, Taryn Burns would like to move the date for the Harvest dinner and have it in a few weeks instead of closer to Thanksgiving. An activity like that may get their minds off the murder."

"That's a wonderful idea." As event coordinator for Spring Hills, Taryn could always find a way to reassure our residents.

Then I remembered something else. "Noreen, we should include something in memory of Pete at our Sunday evening chapel services."

We had chapel service for those who were homebound but still wanted to attend some type of church program. Different pastors from the various churches in Springhill and our own resident retired preacher took turns conducting the service each Sunday. Even though I did attend my own church on Sunday mornings, I was in charge of planning the program each Sunday evening.

"That's a good idea, and I'll leave it up to you as to what to do." She stood. "Now, I need to make a few visits and reassure some of our older, more infirm people that they are safe here."

I left her office and headed for the lounge area to go over my list. First, all those room numbers not facing the courtyard were crossed off. I put a line through Ellie's as she had already said she hadn't seen anything. That left five others. A question mark went beside Jim Tate's name as he's always telling tall tales to anyone who would listen. A great guy, but he was full of himself. Then there was Helen Grayson. A level headed, retired teacher, I could get good information from her if she saw anything.

Tillie McIntosh might talk my arm off before I could get any really usable information, but I'd interview her anyway. Besides, she's the community gossip and knows everything about everybody. She wouldn't hesitate to tell me more than I needed to know and without my even asking.

I eliminated one other name because the poor lady was blind, and her hearing wasn't all that great either. The single person left was Olivia Wentworth, the mother of the chairman of the board and part owner. I thought I might visit with her just because she always seemed so lonely. Mr. Corbin Wentworth might complain and rant when things went wrong, but he seldom made an appearance around here to see his mother.

She occupied a large suite at the end of the hall. Maria and another housekeeper went in and took care of her apartment which had combined two units into one. As soon as the building for memory care was completed, Mrs. Wentworth would be moving there, but for now, her son made sure she had plenty of space in the main building.

Well, that left me with only three people who might be reliable as witnesses. I had to laugh because if the police questioned any of them, the poor officers would give up in frustration with all the other stuff they'd have to listen to. That is if the tenants would even talk to them in the first place.

The next thing would be to see what workers were on duty around that area yesterday. Maybe some of them knew more about Pete and his personal life. I already knew about Maria Roselli, but a good-looking guy like Pete probably had other lady friends.

I glanced at my watch. Oops, I'd have to get busy if I planned to get anything done before lunch. Harry had mentioned going to the police station, so Ben probably went with him. At least one of us should come up with some good information.

I headed down the hall and stopped in at Helen's room. She welcomed me with a smile and an offer of a peppermint from the bowl by her bed. After a few minutes of small talk about the weather, we got down to business.

"Helen, I know your room looks across the lawn. Did you see Pete out there yesterday?"

She raised her eyebrows. "I was wondering if you would get around to asking me about that. I didn't see what happened, but I was late getting dressed yesterday, and when I opened the blinds before I left, I saw him with some woman out there."

"A woman? What did she look like?" That must have happened after I saw him.

"Hmm, well she had dark hair, but I couldn't

see her face. Pete got off his mower to talk with her. She seemed really upset about something because it looked like she was yelling at him. She stomped off, and he went back to work, but that's all I saw. I didn't want to be late for breakfast. I remember she had on a red sweater or jacket and black pants." A frown appeared. "Oh my, I forgot to tell the police that."

"Thank you. I'm sure they'll find that out. If you think of anything else, please let me know."

Out in the hall I stopped and looked at my notes. A dark-haired woman argued with Pete outside. Maria had said she and Pete argued in the employee lounge, and she would have had on her uniform. Could he have had two arguments that day? That seemed weird, but it was the only explanation that fit, and who was the second woman if not Maria? I made notes of questions that needed answering. Find out what other women Pete knew. What did they argue about? How did she get here and where did she go? Looks like I had more to chew on than I could digest for the moment.

Chapter 6

When I headed back toward the lobby, Jim Tate called out to me.

"Hey, Abigail, did you get a new car?"

"Say what? A new car? What gave you that idea Jim?"

He shrugged. "I saw a silver Honda parked behind your house and thought maybe you bought a new one. Then I saw your white one, and it made me wonder why you needed two cars. Did you have a visitor?"

I remembered the car I heard leaving before I took Mitzi outside to play. What if it had been the killer? Whoever killed Pete came and went in a hurry. Why, I could have been an eye-witness myself if I'd been quicker.

Jim crossed his arms and tapped his foot.

"Oh, I'm sorry, my mind wandered a moment. No, I didn't have a visitor, but can you tell me anything else about the car?"

"Not really, but it was gone when I looked out my window later and saw the police arrive." His eyes lit up with excitement. "Say, do you think maybe that was the killer's car?"

Of course I didn't know, but if I said anything Jim would tell everybody he'd seen the killer's car. Who was I kidding? That's exactly what he would do anyway. Maybe I could stall him. "I think it was just somebody visiting, and they had to leave in a hurry."

It sounded lame, but it was all I could think of at the moment. He gave me one of those "Come on now" looks and shook his head.

"Jim, did you see anything else?" Maybe I could get him to thinking in another direction.

"Nope, just noticed the car when I was adjusting my blinds." He turned back to his room then stopped. "Um, I heard Pete and Maria had a thing going. Is that true?"

Now how was I to answer that? I sure don't believe in spreading gossip. "Well, she told me they dated." And that was the truth.

He slapped his thigh. "I knew it. Pretty gal like that is bound to have a good-looking fellow interested in her." Jim laughed then whistled on his way to his apartment.

Why do men think every woman needs a man in her life? I'd done just dandy for the past five years without one, thank you very much. Still, it was kind of nice having Ben pay attention to me. Then I remembered my mission and walked back up the hallway toward Tillie's room. That's when I spotted the tape over the linen closet door lock.

Maria must have forgotten her keys again or hadn't found them. Noreen wasn't going to like that, and it wasn't like Maria to be so careless. I didn't have time to investigate since I still had other names on my list.

The next name on the list belonged to Tillie. I turned toward her apartment, but then I remembered I had told Doris I would come by her place before lunch. Tillie would talk my arm off, and it wasn't like she wouldn't be around whenever I found the chance to find her. Friendship with Doris was more important, and she wouldn't have said anything to me if it wasn't important.

Doris sounded upset and if I neglected her, she would get her feelings hurt and perhaps not confide in me. Since she was usually so quiet, she must have something important to tell me. But then, if I didn't catch the others I wanted to question, they'd be off to lunch and not be back in their rooms for a while.

I sighed. Making my decision, I walked down toward Doris's cottage four houses around the curve from mine. All ten of the independent living cottages formed a large semi-circle at the edge of the wide expanse of lawn down from the main building.

As I strolled to Doris's, I thought about the others. Besides Harry, Ben, Bessie, Doris, Clara, and me, two other singles and two couples lived there. My sleuthing instincts went into gear, and I analyzed the other occupants.

The Stewart's had been out of town all week and didn't even know about Pete yet. Charlie Lewis lived next door to me. I crossed him off. As a former pastor, he was almost like the shepherd of our flock in the cottages. Always looking out for us and taking care of us.

That left the Clays and Edna Burbank. Edna wasn't as big as a minute, so I couldn't see her as a killer, and the Clays were a nice couple. Didn't know them very well since they weren't involved in any of the same activities I was. Ora Mae Clay did have a sense of humor and was quite the comedienne as evidenced by her participation in many of the programs Taryn arranged. Ernest was a like a Teddy Bear and everyone liked him.

Guess that eliminated everyone who lived in these houses, but I might go ahead and question them later. I turned off the walk toward Doris' and realized she had a great view of the golf course and tennis courts.

When I knocked, she peeped through a slit in the door. "Oh, thank goodness, it's you, Abigail." She slipped the chain off and let me inside.

"I hope you don't mind herbal tea. You always drink coffee at breakfast, but I don't even make coffee, so it would probably taste worse than usual."

I perched on one of her barstools. "Tea is fine, Doris." I decided to simply wait for her to get up her courage and tell me what bothered her.

She poured the beverage and set it on the bar with a plate of lemon cookies. Ah, a lady after my own heart. I picked up two of them and placed them on a napkin. Doris chewed on her lip.

Finally, she leaned toward me. "I don't know if what I saw means anything or not, but I have to tell someone, and I'm afraid the police will want to keep questioning me if I tell them."

Her gaze darted from side to side as though she expected someone to jump out from the walls, and her hands shook as she held her cup.

"Oh, Abigail, it was awful. I never said anything to anyone because it's none of my business, but now it takes on new meaning."

I sipped my tea then asked, "What does, Doris?"

"The argument I saw and heard."

I raised my eyebrows. Another argument? It seemed to me like more than a few people had been angry the past few days.

Doris bit her lip again. "I decided to walk down to the tennis courts last week for my daily walk. On my way back, I came by the golf course. I spotted two men out on the first tee. They were gesturing and shouting at each other. I could only hear a few words but it had something to do with being owed what was theirs and not being fair. When I got near, one of them saw me and quieted down. I did hear him say, 'You'll do this over and do it right. This course deserves the best.'"

Hmm, this was interesting news. "Who were the men?"

Her hand clasped the base of her throat. "When I got to them, I saw that it was Pete and Adam, that young man who works in the pro shop and makes out the schedules."

Pete and Adam? Then I remembered how protective Adam could be of that golf course. With so many of the city officials of Springhill playing here, Adam wanted it in the best condition possible. He was probably angry with Pete for not doing a good job. But Pete always took such great pride in his work. I wanted to write this down, but that might cause Doris to clam up. I'd have to rely on my memory for this one.

Doris went on. "I thought Adam was going to hit Pete. In fact, he had his hand raised, but backed off when he saw me. I turned my head and almost ran to my house. When I peeked out through my window, I could still see them up there going at it."

I patted her hand. "Thank you for telling me, Doris. This could be important."

"But, Abigail, they saw it was me. What if Adam killed Pete? He knows I saw them arguing, and if I tell the police, he'll know who told."

"Now, Doris, I don't think you have to worry. Adam wouldn't hurt you." I pondered that a moment. If Adam was capable of killing Pete, he might be angry enough to harm Doris.

"But just in case, I'll ask Harry to keep an eye on your place. He can stop by here and walk with you to meals. And you can call me if you want to go anywhere else." I squeezed her hand and offered my usual tried and true solution. "Let's pray about it."

We bowed our heads, and I held her hands. "Lord, I come to you this morning seeking Your hedge of protection about my friend Doris. Keep her safe and remove her fears. We know Your love and power will work to all that is good for Doris. In Your name we pray. Amen."

She sat back with relief. "Oh, thank you. I know the Lord will take care of me." Doris jumped up. "Won't you stay for lunch?"

I hated to say no, but more important things needed my attention, and this new information needed to be added to what we already had. "Thank you for the invitation, but I have some business to take care of. I'll see you at dinner."

I left and headed back to the main building. Good thing it had been Doris who had seen the altercation. If it had been Bessie, she would've marched right up there and tried to stop it. Clara would've shouted at them and then called Noreen Jenson to report it. Of course, the latter may have kept Pete from being murdered. As Alice would say, things were getting "curiouser and curiouser."

I arrived at my cottage and stopped. I added Adam to my mental list of people to question, and that made three different people arguing with Pete. If he had that many upset with him, we'd have our hands full trying to figure out what happened.

I'd see Adam this afternoon at the pro shop when I checked in for my golf round. I glanced at my watch. Since Ben and Harry hadn't returned, I decided to question the grounds manager even though they were to take care of questioning the men. I had thirty minutes left before everyone stopped for lunch. Maybe I could catch him down at the garden center.

The walk ate up four precious minutes, but I found Tom Kirk in his office. I rapped on the door frame, and he beckoned me in.

"I figured I might be seeing you or one of your friends soon. With Pete found in your flower bed, I knew you'd want out to find out who did it." His grin spread across his face, and his words were like butter melting on a hot biscuit.

If he thought I was just a meddling old woman, he had another thought coming. "Why wouldn't I be interested in Pete's murder? It took place beside my cottage. How well did you know Pete?" Now that sounded like a dumb question. Exactly how much did he actually know about his own employees?

"Pete's been on the crew for five years. He's a—was a good worker. I've never had any complaints."

"Not even about the greens on the golf course?"

He narrowed his eyes. "Have you been talking to Adam? He's a perfectionist where his golf course is concerned. I think he got down on his hands and knees and inspected every blade after Pete mowed."

That's why we had the best golf course in the county if not the whole northwest corner of the state. Even the Razorback golf team came over for practice on our layout. I never found any fault with it, but then I wasn't an expert.

"No, I haven't talked with Adam. I know he can be a pain, but our fairways and greens always looked good to me. And Pete was always willing to take extra time to help me with my plants and shrubs."

Tom Kirk nodded. "Yeah, Pete was like that. He enjoyed helping people. I think that's why he was so upset that Maria wouldn't let him give her the money to help pay for some of her daughter's medical expenses."

My head almost jerked back. "Oh, you know about that? I understand they had quite an argument about it."

"Pete came to me that morning and wanted me to see if there was a way to get it to Mrs. Jensen and have her give it to Maria as a bonus. I said I'd look into it, but then I never got the chance." His fist hit the desk. "I lost me one good man, and he'll be hard to replace."

"I'm sure he will." I glanced down at my notes. Oh, yes, Pete's background. "Do you know of any debts Pete may have had?"

"Yes and no. He told me he got into trouble over some gambling debts he racked up in one of the Oklahoma casinos, but he took care of it with that big win he bragged about around here. I don't know of any since then."

I started to mention the arrests, but couldn't remember the details of them. I knew the corporation did a thorough background check of all employees before hiring. I'd have to go back and check that information with Harry.

I tried another avenue. "Pete was such a good-looking man. Do you know if he had any other girlfriends besides Maria?" I cringed a little when I realized what I was doing was tantamount to gossip and hearsay, but I waited for his answer.

"Umm, I do know he dated other staff members, but I don't think any of them were serious until Maria. Some seemed to think Pete was a womanizer, but if so, it didn't affect his job as a top-notch gardener." Then he shoved back from his desk. "Sorry, I've said too much already. I haven't even told the police what I've told you."

When I looked askance at him, he quickly added, "Only because they didn't ask me specifically about other women." Then he offered his hand across the desk. "I don't know what it is about you, Mrs. Billings, but you do know the right questions to ask."

I stood and shook his hand. "Well, I appreciate your honesty." And I did, but I sure wished I knew which staff members Pete had dated before Maria. I'd have to do more snooping with employees. Then I remembered Tillie. If anyone would know, she would. I'd have to pay her that visit I missed earlier. She'd be more likely to give me a straight answer than any of the other men on the grounds crew.

Chapter 7

My stomach growled to remind me lunchtime had arrived. I hurried back to my house and fixed a ham sandwich. I added some chips, a soft drink, and a handful of chocolate chip cookies to the plate and sat down to enjoy my meal before meeting Ben and Harry.

Tillie had a stroke not long ago, but with her therapy sessions she had really improved. She is two years older than I am and has the courage and stamina of one much younger. She was also sharp as a tack, and not much escaped her eyes or ears. It should be an interesting visit.

After eating and taking care of Mitzi, I headed out for my round of golf. I hope Ben might decide to keep our date and join me, but that was wishful thinking. I did wait, just in case, but when he didn't show, I went on without him. If he came, he'd have to catch-up.

I didn't see Adam before I teed off, but when I finished nine holes and returned to the pro shop, Adam was at the counter.

"Oh, hi, Mrs. Billings, I didn't see you come in. Ben Martin called earlier and said he couldn't make the golf date today. Sorry I wasn't here to give you the message."

That Ben. Wonder what his excuse will be this time. Never mind him now, I needed some information. I purchased a new bag of tees. "You take such pride in everything to do with the course. I bet you'll miss Pete taking care of it."

His ears reddened like they'd been sunburned, and he hesitated before answering. "Yes, it's a shame what happened to him."

"He always did such a wonderful job. It sure made my game a lot better. He'll be missed."

Adam's eyebrows shot up and his apple bobbled in his throat. "Yes, he will."

I hefted my golf bag to my shoulder. "I'll see you at my usual tee time day after tomorrow." This young man had something to hide.

He jotted down my name on the schedule and I left. A few yards away, I stopped and glanced back. Sure enough, he was staring at me, but he swirled around in a hurry to get something from the shelf when he realized I was looking. I was sure he hadn't told me the whole truth.

Harry was to meet me after my golf game. If Ben came with him, I might give him a piece of my mind for standing me up. Tillie would have to wait again, but then she didn't even expect me to visit anyway.

When I arrived home, I put the coffee on to drip and brought out the blueberry muffins I'd made last night.

While waiting for the men to arrive, I went back over all the information gleaned this morning. Three arguments in two days, and it appeared that all three people had been angry with Pete. Two had been identified, Maria and Adam, but not that mysterious third woman. Who was the black-haired woman in the red sweater and black pants? I didn't recall seeing anyone dressed in those colors that day, but then I hadn't seen everyone who lives or works here or even noticed what they were wearing.

Adam may have been upset about something Pete didn't do on the golf course, but could it have been motive enough for murder? Adam would have the opportunity, but I couldn't see him hitting Pete over the head. Maria admitted her argument, but Pete had been trying to do something for her, so where was her motive?

Both Adam and Maria had opportunity with their free access to the area, but that third argument most intrigued me at the moment. If I found her, then both motive and opportunity might be discovered. Then again, that silver car couldn't be counted out.

Ben and Harry finally arrived. I scowled at Ben. "Where were you this afternoon?"

"Um, I had things to do. Sorry, maybe next time."

Harry headed for my computer. "I have something to show you. Pete had more than one website."

I prepared a tray with cups of coffee and a basket of muffins and set it on the small table in the living room.

Harry suddenly yelled out. "Here it is. Come look."

Ben hurried to Harry's side. "What did you

find?"

He grinned. "I decided do a little more searching on Pete after I left here."

I peered at the screen. "Why, that's Pete and one of the other attendants. Steve, I think. He's the one who takes Ellie to the church services on Sunday evenings when he's on duty. What are he and Pete doing with web pages?"

Harry glanced up at me. "It's another website similar to the one I showed you earlier, but it's a different because this one is a blog. The other one was mostly about gardening tips, but this one is more of a blog about himself and Steve. It's sort of a journal where people talk about different things. Blog is short for 'web log.'" Harry scrolled down the screen.

I leaned closer. I had seen the one earlier, but since I didn't know about blogs, I wasn't really sure what I was looking at.

Harry scrolled down. "It looks like he and Steve won big in Oklahoma a while back and they're bragging about it. Then it looks like they won again. In his last entry, he and Steve are bragging about how their luck changed and how they're going to win more in the future."

"Now that seems strange. I know he and Steve won big not long ago because of the way Steve went on about it, and Pete also wanted to help Maria, but why put all that on the computer?" I stepped back from the machine and reached over to get my notebook from the desk.

"Because people like to brag and talk about their successes. He doesn't say where they won the money except in Oklahoma."

Harry had scrolled down more. "Hmm, he and Steve both contribute to this blog. They both talk about the casinos and their winnings over in Oklahoma. They hint at a scheme they have for beating the house." He paused a moment. "If you ask me, these boys are begging for trouble by posting this where anybody and everybody can see it."

I read through some of what appeared on the screen. "I can't believe the arrogance I see here. Listen to this, Ben.

"Pete and I won big last week at the Black Jack tables. Pete took our money, invested it and came up with double our winnings. His plan is working. We're going to try it out on a trip to Vegas. If it works there, we'll be on our way. We'll show them a thing or two. If you're interested, leave a comment below."

Harry pointed to some responses below the article. "These are the people who made comments about it and want to know more about their scheme."

Ben shook his head and leaned back in the recliner. "This looks like a dangerous road for the two of them and a good motive for murder."

Harry clicked on the printer to copy a few pages. "I'm thinking the same thing, and this may be bigger than either of us can handle, Ben."

What about me? I was in on this, too, and I'd show them. "Not so fast, let me tell you what happened this morning." I proceeded to tell them about Pete's two new arguments.

Harry let out a low whistle. "Our Pete sure had his share of enemies."

I picked up our empty cups to take them to the kitchen. "Or just people who were angry or upset with him. I can't see any of them as motives. I haven't talked to anyone about who the other woman could be, but I just know he dated some of the staff other than Maria. Tillie is on my list to interview before dinner. If there's anything to be known, she'll know it."

"That's a good idea. She may be nosy, but in this case, it'll help." Ben stood and stretched. "As much as I like the company, I'm going home to rest a little before I eat."

Harry gathered up pages he'd printed out. "You do that, and I'll head on down to my place and do some more computer searching. I'll see you two at dinner."

"I'll go on back and find Tillie. Maybe we'll have more to report tonight." At least I hoped Tillie would have more information.

They left, and I went to rescue Mitzi and take her outdoors for a few minutes. I secured her leash to a post so she could be in the fresh air but not able to run away and get into trouble. From there I hurried over to the main building.

Carrie sat at her desk in the foyer when I arrived. She didn't look up at my greeting, and I barely heard her response. When I asked her about Tillie, she pointed in the direction of the library.

How strange that she wouldn't even look at me. What could be that important? She even looked as though she wished I'd leave, so I went to search for

Tillie. Sure enough, she sat in a corner chair in the library engrossed in the book she held. On closer inspection, she read one of the new cozy mysteries we get for our collection every month from a publisher.

"Hello, Tillie."

She jumped and dropped her book. "Oh my, Abigail, you scared me out of my wits."

I picked up the book. "Sorry, you've lost your place."

"That's okay. I know exactly where I was." She glanced at the book, turned a few pages then inserted the book mark. She peered up at me with questions written all over her face.

If I didn't get right to the point, she'd be hounding me for any information I might have concerning Pete. I pulled a chair over closer to her.

"Tillie, you're very knowledgeable about what goes on around Spring Hills, and I need your help."

Her eyes opened wide. "Is this about Pete? That poor man. He may have been a gambler and a ladies' man, but he didn't deserve to die like that."

Aha! Pay-dirt. Tillie wanted to talk. Now to tread softly so her feelings wouldn't be hurt. Last thing I wanted was for her to think we all thought she was a nosy gossip.

"Pete was a handsome man. I'm sure he had lots of women interested in him."

Tillie nodded. "Oh, that he did. Love and leave 'em was his style. Why he broke poor Taryn Burns' heart a few months ago before he took up with Maria, that housekeeper."

"Taryn Burns? I didn't know about that."

Maybe she was who Tom Kirk meant earlier this morning.

"Oh, it was supposed to be a secret, but I saw them together several times and put one and one together and came up with a couple. That's how I knew he was seeing Maria, too. I think he'd been seeing Carrie and one of the nurses, too. He really got around."

Sure she did. Tillie always seemed to be in the right place at the right time to learn all sorts of information. Then I remembered my other question.

"Did you see anything unusual across the yard toward my house yesterday morning?"

"Come to think of it, I did. There was a gray car behind your house near your car. I thought maybe you had a visitor. Pete was mowing out there when Taryn stopped him and they argued something fierce. He turned away and she followed him."

Now this was getting somewhere. "What was she wearing?"

"Hmm, I believe she had on a red sweater and black pants. I saw her later in the game room and that's what she had on, but she left just after that. Said she had the day off."

Bingo. My mystery woman was Taryn. "What happened then?"

"Oh, Olivia Wentworth popped in. You know how she's always roaming around. I asked her what she needed, and she said she couldn't find her dining room. Well, I decided to help her and then forgot all about Taryn and Pete."

Well, pooh. No new information, but now I did

have a name for the second woman seen with Pete. "Umm, what do you know about Steve?"

"Oh, he and Pete were gambling buddies. They were always talking about some scheme to strike it rich at the gaming tables. I think they went over to the casinos just about every week-end they were off. He used to play poker too."

Now how did she know all that? I'd just found out that myself. I hesitated to ask, but didn't have to worry about that as Tillie kept on talking without any prompting.

"Sometimes I think the employees around here think we're all old and senile. It's amazing what you can learn in this building if you watch and listen. I may be weak in the body from my stroke, but my eyes and ears are as good as they ever were. Pete would come in at lunch and talk with Steve once in a while. One time, Steve was helping me by moving a piece of furniture when Pete stopped by, and they talked about a poker game. I sat over in the corner quiet as a mouse pretending to be interested in a book I picked up."

Tillie had a lot more going on in her brain than any of us gave her credit for. She may talk a person's arm off, but she knew how to get information. "Reading a book was a smart idea."

Tillie grinned. "I thought so too. Anyway, Steve talked about winning big at the casino last month and wanting his share of the money, but Pete told him they'd have to wait on that. He had plans to use what they had and make more. Steve got a bit angry at that, but Pete calmed him down."

So, Steve had issues with Pete, too. Seems to

me Pete had made a lot of enemies in the past few weeks. A glance at my notes reminded me that we had a full plate of suspects and little time to digest all the information. However, I could cross off Steve because he was on vacation according to the staff schedule posted in Noreen's office.

I couldn't believe Tillie knew so much that was going on in the main building. Maybe I'd better spend more time up here. A lot happened that some of us didn't have any idea about. Tillie must be the source of all Bessie's knowledge too.

Tillie probably had more to say, but I should get back to check to make a record of all she told me. Before she could offer to tell me more, we heard quite a commotion from the area of the main entrance. Tillie was out of her chair like a shot and grabbed her walker before I could even think to move. That woman may be recovering from a stroke, but she could get around when she wanted to.

Chapter 8

When we entered the lobby, Maria and Noreen were in a heated discussion. Maria sobbed, and Noreen looked fit to be tied.

"I'm sorry, Mrs. Jensen, but my keys just disappeared. I had them when I put my things away in my locker, and then I had that argument with Pete. I don't know what happened to them after that."

"Why didn't you report it immediately instead of telling Carrie you left them at home?"

"I . . . I thought maybe I'd been mistaken about having them with me. I was so upset with Pete's murder, I couldn't think straight. I searched everywhere at home and couldn't find them, so I don't know what happened or where they are."

Noreen shook her head. "This is not good. If anyone took them or found them or stole them or whatever, it could be real trouble for all of us. I don't want to fire you because we're shorthanded as it is, but if we don't find those keys, I may have to. In the meantime, I'll issue you another set."

"Yes, ma'am, I understand. I'll look everywhere around here and at home again."

Noreen nodded and turned to leave. She spotted me and shook her head again. "I guess you heard all that."

"Yes, I did. It's strange how the keys disappeared on the same morning Pete was murdered."

"I don't know what to think. I know you're talking to the residents, so maybe you could add this to your list. Maybe someone saw her keys and picked them up but forgot to turn them."

That seemed unlikely to me, but I'd give it a go. "All right, I will." Ben and Harry would need to know about this new development as well.

"Thank you. Now I need to see to getting her more keys." She headed down the hall toward her office.

Tillie had gone over to console Marie, so I headed back home. When I exited the building, I ran into Ben and Harry.

Ben peered over my shoulder. "What's going on in there? I see Tillie with her arm around Marie."

I explained the situation to them both while we walked back to my cottage.

Ben shrugged and let out his breath. "She's probably laid them down somewhere and forgotten about it. I'm sure they'll turn up soon."

We stopped at my place and Harry held some papers. "I was on my way down to the station to check on the progress of the investigation. Thought I'd show them some of the stuff I've found on Pete's blog. They might have already seen this, but it won't hurt to show them."

"Sounds like a good idea. I'm going to take

Mitzi for her walk. Mealtime is only half an hour away. Will you two be there?"

With reassurance he'd be there, Harry waved and walked on toward his own place. Ben stayed behind. He must want something, so I waited for him to speak his mind.

All three of us had been working on this case, and it seems we were getting nowhere. Pete had lovers' quarrels, debts because of gambling, and bragging because of some big scheme for winning. We needed to focus more on his relationship with Steve.

As though reading my mind, Ben said, "Do we know for certain Steve is out of town?"

"Of course not, how would we?" I stepped up on my porch and opened my door. "I have to take care of Mitzi, so I'll see you later."

He waved and walked down to his house and I headed around to the back to let Mitzi back into the house. She jumped all over me when I unfastened the leash. My poor baby didn't like me being gone hours at a time. The crime scene tape had been removed, so I let her loose to run about the yard instead of taking a walk.

I followed her around the corner and discovered her digging in the dirt under my bedroom window. I was sure glad the tape had been removed, or we'd be in big trouble. "Mitzi quit that digging and come here."

She raised her head to give me a "not now" look and went back to digging. I marched over to her and reached for her. Before I could grab her, she shook her head, and something dangled from her mouth.

I grabbed them and realized I was holding Maria's keys. How in the world had they ended up here? I hugged Mitzi to my chest. "Good girl, good girl. Now let's get inside and get you cleaned up."

If there had been any other prints on those keys besides Maria's, I'd ruined them if Mitzi hadn't. After cleaning her paws of the mud and dirt, I cleaned up for dinner. I'd take the keys with me and give them to Noreen if she hadn't left already.

Conversation this evening hummed, but at a much softer tone than last night and breakfast this morning. Clara, Doris, and Bessie sat alone at our table with heads bent toward each other. When I sat down, they straightened up and busied their hands with napkins and silverware. Bessie finally looked at me.

"Where are Ben and Harry?"

"I don't know. I expected to see them here." At that moment, I spotted Noreen out in the lobby. "Excuse me ladies, I must speak to Noreen before she leaves."

I caught up with her at the reception desk where Carrie had gathered up her things to leave for the day. "Noreen, look what I found." I held up the keys.

Carrie gasped behind me, and when I turned around, she looked away, but not before I noticed her pale face. She left in a rush without saying good-bye.

Noreen grabbed the keys. "Where in the world did you find them?"

"Out in the flower bed where Pete was—well

actually, Mitzi dug them up."

Noreen's eyes opened wide and she inhaled a deep breath. "This doesn't look good for Maria."

"I wouldn't be so sure. The crime scene investigators searched the area before they removed the tape. They would have found them if they were there when Pete was killed."

"Maybe you're right. In any case, I'll get them back to Maria tomorrow and tell her to be more careful."

She took the keys and headed back to her office.

I was pretty sure Maria hadn't put them there because I believed her when she said she and Pete argued in the employee lounge, and she certainly wasn't any of the women described by others. I would make it a point to speak with Maria tomorrow.

When I returned to the table, the three women were at it again with heads bent toward each other. Ben and Harry arrived right after I sat down.

The three women straightened up and quit talking. I glared at Bessie. "All right, I know something's up. What were you talking about?"

Bessie's cheeks turned even redder than the blush she usually wore. She glanced from Clara to Doris before turning to me. "We were just discussing how many quarrels Pete had the morning he was murdered and before. Adam, Steve, Maria, some mystery woman, and even someone in a gray car parked behind your house. It's obvious that one of those people is the killer. Steve may not have gone out of town, and he could have come back here, killed Pete and left before anyone saw him. That mystery woman could have done it and left in that gray car. Someone said he also had another girlfriend here before Maria and Taryn, so she could have done it as well."

How in the world had Bessie come up with so much information? I had questioned at least three if not four people to get all that. She and Tillie must have been talking. I glanced at Ben and Harry. Both of their faces wore stunned expressions.

The old game of Gossip from childhood came to mind. We loved to play it at parties and the story told at the end rarely matched the one started before making its way through five or six teen girls. I was sure the stories these women repeated had gone through a number of versions and revisions and had little to do with actuality although they did bear a thread of the truth.

"You ladies have been watching way too much TV." Their minds needed to go in a different direction. "I don't know where you got all that information, but it's all a lot of speculation. Let's forget about that and talk about the tournaments coming up. Harry and I plan to win the Bridge tournament no matter how hard you and Ben try to beat us."

That got Bessie's mind going to another topic. "Really, you think you can win? The last two have been ours and will be again." She smiled, and her dimples flashed. "Isn't that so, Ben?"

"You can count on it." He stared at me with that smirk of his.

He was angry with me for choosing Harry as

my partner, but I didn't care. Both men had analytical minds and were great partners. I just didn't want to encourage Ben into thinking we might have a relationship. With three tournaments a year, Harry and I were bound to win one.

Conversation returned to the normal topics of contests and trivia. I finished my dinner and prepared to leave. "If you will excuse me, I'm heading home to Mitzi. I'll see you in the morning." I sure used her as an excuse for a lot of things I wanted to do.

Ben raised his eyebrows, and I nodded to let him know I'd be waiting for him and Harry at my house.

Mitzi jumped all over me when I opened the door to let her out. I secured her leash and took her outdoors for a few minutes. No way would I let her run free this evening in the dark even if we are well-lighted.

After we went back inside, I put on a pot of coffee. With all the activity of the past few days, I hadn't had time to do any baking, so the boys would have to get by on coffee alone.

In less than five minutes they arrived and settled themselves at the table. I filled three mugs and set them on the table.

"Today I learned a lot goes on around here that I didn't know about. We need to get up to the main building more often and sit in on some of those group activities." I relayed all the information from Jim and Tillie as well as what Doris had told me.

Ben let out a low whistle. "That *is* a lot of information, and the ladies at dinner weren't far from the truth." He set his mug down. "Get your pad and let's go over what we know and how it might tie together."

I retrieved my notepad and picked up a pen. "Okay, we know Maria had an argument with Pete over money, Adam and Pete had a disagreement about an unknown subject because I don't think it had anything to do with the lawn, and Steve argued with Pete regarding their gambling."

I wrote each name and comment on the pad. "Taryn had an argument out in yard by my house, so she's a suspect, and we can't forget that gray or silver car Jim saw and I heard leaving."

Ben leaned over and turned the list toward him. "Looks like they all have a motive and the opportunity except maybe Maria who didn't leave the building although the keys in the flowerbed slants suspicion in her direction."

Harry sat back and pressed his fingertips together. "We need to start eliminating people by checking alibis. That means making sure Steve really went out of town for vacation and learning more about the mystery car."

He pulled a piece of paper from his shirt pocket. "Here's a little more I learned about Pete this afternoon. Steve and Pete were definitely partners in a casino scheme. We knew he went to the casinos, but from this entry a last week, it looks like he won quite big which matches what we read from earlier. He read the entry aloud.

"We cleaned up with Blackjack. We're investing some of the money but we plan to go back and win even more as we've learned a system. With our next big win, we'll have no more debts and lots of fun." He laid paper on the table.

"Then Steve adds his part about the things he'll do with his winnings."

"That must be what Tillie heard him talking about with Pete. He did say something about a scheme to make even more. Wonder if that had anything to do with the murder? From what I'd heard, men are all the time trying to find ways to beat the bank."

Ben shook his head. "That's break the bank, Abby."

"Whatever. Anyway, maybe he came up with another plan for winning at poker, too. Too bad Steve is on vacation." I picked up the pad again.

"That still leaves the mystery car."

Harry folded the paper with the info about Pete and Steve. "I'll check that out again because if those boys were mixed up in a scheme like that, they may have attracted the attention of the casino owners where they won so big. If that's the case, we may have more than we can handle, and we'll need to give all our information to the police."

"I agree, so let's sleep on it and go over what we know in the morning." Ben stood and picked up his jacket. "I'm heading home. Are you coming, Harry?"

"Yeah, I'll join you. Thanks for the coffee, and we'll see you at breakfast."

They left, and I pondered the information we had. Somewhere in it all lay the answer, but would we recognize it if we found it?

Chapter 9

On Friday, the police had returned or rather that detective had and questioned me as well as a few others again. This time I remembered to tell him about the gray or silver car that had roared away that morning. He didn't appear too happy that I hadn't told him before now, but I blamed it on my memory.

Tillie had been in a tizzy after she'd been questioned and told me she wasn't sure what she'd told him. I told her it was okay and not to worry about it. The detective would take care of sorting it all out.

Noreen had been out ill yesterday, so he'd probably be back to question her later. Taryn handled everything, but I never got the chance to talk with her. She had her own as well as Noreen's responsibilities yesterday, but they'd be here today.

I pondered this on my way to breakfast on Saturday. Pete's memorial in our chapel was scheduled for tomorrow night, but no one had given us any information about an actual funeral or burial. Noreen had said she'd let us know as soon as she knew anything. With her being off on weekends, I'd have to wait until Monday to ask any questions.

Before going to the dining hall, I headed for Taryn's office to talk about the plans for tomorrow night. I also wanted to question her about her relationship with Pete. Taryn had always been one of my favorites at Spring Hill, but after the information from yesterday, that could change. This was the perfect time to question her. Before I could knock on her door, she stepped into the hall.

"Oh, Abigail, you're the one I wanted to see this morning. Is everything all set for the memorial service tomorrow night?"

"Yes, everything is set. This must be difficult for you since I was told you went out to talk to him the day he died."

Her face blanched, and she blinked her eyes as though to stop tears. "Yes, I did. It's awful to think I may have been the last person to see him before the person who killed him."

"I understand you two once were in a relationship. Is that right?"

Taryn fingered the papers in her arms and blew out her breath. "We had a few dates, but it didn't go far. We were more friends than lovers. Before breakfast was the only time I could catch him to ask a favor. I asked him if he'd get some fresh flower arrangements for Mrs. Simpson's birthday party in a few weeks. Her family is having a reception for her old friends from her church. He said he'd didn't have time, and he still had to order the ones for the banquet coming up."

It all sounded logical. Still, there was the fact Helen said she saw them arguing as did Tillie. "That must have upset you. Someone told me you were arguing with him."

She looked down at her feet and shook her head. "Eyes and ears are all over this place." Then she glanced back at me. "Yes, I did argue with him. After he said he didn't have time to worry about flowers for some party for an old lady, and he hadn't ordered the other ones, I reminded him that he was the only one who could get the flowers I wanted to use this time of year. He can—could be so stubborn at times."

Her eyes actually misted over. "I'm not sure what we'll do now about the decorations." She shook her head. "That's why I was looking for you."

"Me. How can I help?"

We walked back toward the main reception area as she explained. "Noreen and I both think you're the perfect one to head up the decorations. Maybe Mr. Kirk can get the flowers for us, but we thought you and your friends could help take care of decorating the room and the tables for us."

My mind whirled with all the things suddenly happening. I had a list of suspects and questions for Pete's murder and now this. However, I couldn't turn her down. "I'll do what I can. Our residents need something to cheer them up and get their minds off this tragedy."

"Thank you so much, Abigail. You'll do a great job. Oh, and I also need to know what you have on tap for the memorial. I sing in the choir at my church on Sunday evenings, but I called in an excuse, so I could attend."

Then I remembered the solo she sang at one of

our Sunday services not long ago, and how I had admired her beautiful soprano voice. "Oh, Taryn, could you sing a special number at the service?"

She hesitated a moment and bit her lip. "I suppose I could. What would you want?"

"How about *How Great Thou Art* like you sang for us not long ago? We have *Amazing Grace* as a group hymn."

"I could do that. Doesn't Clara Bivens play the piano for your services? I can get with her and practice later today."

"She does, and I know she'd be delighted to accompany you."

We stopped at the reception desk. "Carrie, we may have guests come in tomorrow night for Pete's memorial. Please make sure they have their name tags before coming to the chapel."

Carrie's face paled and her hands shook. "Yes, Miss Ryan. I'll make sure."

I studied Carrie a moment while she talked with Taryn. Carrie worked every other week-end, and this happened to be the one she would be on duty. Everyone who came in had to register with Carrie before going to the chapel or to any of the care areas.

Her face gave me pause. Every time I or someone else had mentioned Pete this week, she'd reacted in a rather strange way. Had she been another one of his girlfriends? That would make this whole case even more complicated and confusing.

Taryn finished her conversation with Carrie and turned back to me. "Noreen is off, but Mrs. Fuller is here if you need anything from her, and

I'm going back to my office."

After Taryn left, Carrie's hands still trembled when she shuffled the papers on her desk.

"You seem distracted today, Carrie. Is there anything I can help you with?"

"Oh, no, Ma'am, it's all this business with that detective being here and questioning people again."

I didn't believe her, but then a detective nosing around would be disconcerting. "All right then, I'll see you after a while." The aromas from the dining hall reminded me of my purpose for being in the building.

Conversation hummed as usual, and at our table, the topic revolved around Bridge games again. Sometimes I wonder if Bessie had anything else but bridge or gossip she deems worthy of conversation.

After breakfast, Ben followed me outside. "What are your plans for the day?"

"Visit a few more people and ask more questions. Olivia Wentworth will be my first stop. She's the only one I haven't talked to on that wing."

Ben glanced at his watch. "I'd like to go with you to see Olivia. Her dementia seems to be getting worse."

"All right. She should be finished with her breakfast by now, and yes, she is getting more and more forgetful."

Her son, Trenton, had finally admitted his mother's Alzheimer's disease. That was the main reason for the building of the Memory Care Unit. It would be finished sometime next year, but until then, Olivia lived in her larger first floor apartment.

A few minutes later, we knocked on her door. When she opened it, her eyes appeared confused for a moment. She peered over my shoulder at Ben and frowned.

Ben stepped forward. "Good morning, Mrs. Wentworth. I'm Ben Martin and this is Abby Billings. We just came by to say hello."

Recognition replaced confusion and a broad smile lit up the elderly lady's face. "Oh, do come in. I don't have many visitors, and this is a pleasure."

Ben followed me into the room and we sat down with her in her living area. I gazed around at the furnishings and recognized them as fine antiques. The rich dark woods gleamed in the light from crystal lamps adorned with silk shades.

Then I realized she had spoken to me. "I'm sorry, Mrs. Wentworth. I was admiring your beautiful home."

"Oh, please call me Olivia." Her hand swept through the air. "These are some of my most favorite pieces. Mr. Wentworth bought them for me."

At this moment Olivia seemed to be perfectly lucid and completely in control. I had difficulty imagining this dear lady being lost, but I had seen it with my own eyes. However, this visit would probably go down as just a nice morning with a lovely lady. But why did she refer to her son as *Mr. Wentworth?*

I leaned forward. "Olivia, are you planning to attend Pete's memorial service tomorrow evening?"

Confusion filled Olivia's eyes. "I'm sorry. I don't know about any party. I wasn't invited."

"Oh, but everyone's invited. It'll be right here in our prayer chapel."

Olivia shook her head. "Oh, my dear, you must be mistaken. There's no party here tomorrow. I haven't sent out invitations or planned a menu or anything. I'll have to speak to Mr. Wentworth about this."

Suddenly the reference dawned on me. Olivia thought she was in her own home, and Mr. Wentworth must be her husband. But he'd been dead for many years.

Olivia peered up at Ben. "Now who are you? And why are you here?"

Ben moved to Olivia's side. "I'm Ben Martin, and we came for a visit. I live at Spring Hills."

Olivia clasped her hands together in her lap. "I think my son owns that place. I've heard the name somewhere." Suddenly she stood. "I'm not minding my manners. May I get you a cup of tea?"

I shook my head. "No, thank you, I'm fine." I stood and motioned for Ben to do the same. "It's been pleasant visiting with you, Mrs. Wentworth. We'll come back when we have more time to visit."

She accompanied us to the door. "I'm sorry, you can't stay longer. Please do come back. I'm worried about safety ever since that gardener was murdered."

Now she was back in the present. Maybe she knew something after all. "Yes, that was a terrible thing."

"A number of things went on. A woman talked to him and some man came up the way a bit. He drove a silver car."

That car again. "What did he look like?"

"Big and brawny." She nodded her head and pointed at Ben. "Bigger than this man who came with you."

How could she have seen him so well from this distance? "Did you notice what he was wearing?"

"Not really. He wasn't wearing a suit, but he had on some type of dark jacket like a windbreaker."

Not sure how much that would help, but it was a lot more than I had before. At the door, I extended a hand toward the older woman. "Thank you for allowing us to visit with you. You are a gracious hostess."

Olivia beamed. "You're welcome. You and your friend can come back any time."

I nodded. "That would be nice."

Ben stepped out into the hall. Olivia snapped her fingers. "Those numbers I saw were 555-LQR and they were red and white." Then she closed the door.

"What on earth was that?"

Ben shook his head. "I'm not sure, but it may have been a license plate number."

"I think you're right. Arkansas plates are white with red and are a combination of letters and numbers just like that." Her strange behavior did raise doubts, but stranger things have happened.

Ben shook his head. "The poor woman doesn't know where she is. And she's so proud of everything in her home. One minute she knew exactly what she was saying and doing, and then the next I was a complete stranger."

"I know, and I believe her son was right in saying she may be suffering from Alzheimer's.

"If you think it's worth a try, I'll give those numbers to Harry, and let him check it out."

"Thank you, it may come to naught, but it can't hurt." No sense in giving them to the police until we knew if there was a connection to Pete.

When we left the building, Ben turned towards the cottages and Harry's place. I planned to make another visit with Ellie. I had neglected her for a few days, and she needed to know I hadn't forgotten her.

I kept thinking about poor Olivia. Ben was right. There was no way an elderly lady like Olivia could have seen the license plate on the car in my driveway from that distance. Probably another wild goose chase, but then again, stranger things had led to solving crimes.

Chapter 10

S unday evening, we gathered in the chapel for our regular evening service, but tonight it would be a special time of memory for Pete. Our own resident Pastor Lewis conducted the service this week.

We sang a few old hymns we all love, and just before his message, Pastor Lewis said a few words about Pete.

"Pete Graham loved the earth and working in it. Many times, we spoke of nature and God's creation. One of his great prides was in the beauty of our grounds here at Spring Hills. No matter what task any one of us requested regarding our own gardening, he took it on and did his best. He's the reason behind Mrs. Billings' beautiful azaleas each year and the lovely rose garden we all enjoy.

"Pete believed in the Lord, but like all humans, he had his faults. Despite those, he was a good man, and one whom we will all miss. His mother called me this afternoon, and Pete's funeral service will be Tuesday afternoon at two. There will be a van available to take any of you who would like to attend and don't want to drive. And now, Miss Taryn Ryan will sing for us in Pete's memory."

Taryn's lovely soprano voice sang out the words to *How Great Thou Art*. My heart soared with the melody, and I realized anew how great our God is. When she finished, we all sat in silent appreciation of a song well-done. Pastor Lewis brought a short message on forgiveness and love, and then we were dismissed.

A number of our residents gathered around Taryn to compliment her solo. Her smile lit up her face, and I could see why any man would be attracted to her. I would add her to my prayer list for her to find the right man for her life.

Ben nudged my arm. "I would never have believed Taryn could sing like that."

"She's a member of the choir at her church, and she's sung before for us. That's why I suggested she sing tonight."

"Very good choice, which leads me to believe she's not our killer despite the fact she did argue with Pete."

"I've come to the same conclusion." I nodded toward Harry. "See if you can get him out of the grips of Bessie and come down to my place. We need to discuss this some more."

"I'll do that. See you in a bit." He strolled over to Harry, and I made my way outside and down the walk to my cottage. My cell phone jingled its merry tune.

Bessie's voice came on when I answered, and she didn't sound happy at all.

"Abigail Billings, Ben just canceled our practice Bridge game for tonight. What's this all about? I've seen you and him and Harry with your heads together. What's going on?"

"I'm sorry Ben canceled. I didn't know you were due a practice session when I invited him for coffee and a piece of pie. I'll tell him we can do this some other time and send him back."

Her exasperated sigh came over the airwave loud and clear. "No, that won't be necessary. As long as you and Harry aren't going over strategy, we'll be okay. I'll see you at breakfast. Good-bye."

The call ended, and I slipped the phone back into my pocket. If Bessie knew what we were really doing, she'd have a hissy-fit and want to be included. If we did that, she'd be spreading the word faster than greased lightning. I wouldn't bet on any contest pitting her against Tillie for letting people know what was going on, but then most of Bessie's information came from Tillie anyway.

After the coffee started dripping, I went out the back way with Mitzi and let her off the leash for a few minutes. A car now sat in the carport of the Stewart cottage, so they must have returned from their trip. That got me to thinking again about that silver or gray car. If we knew who had been driving it, we would have another suspect and a good one at that.

Mitzi bounded around the corner and stopped at my feet. She dropped something on the ground, sat back on her haunches, and tilted her head. I leaned down to pick it up and found an earring.

I held it a moment because I had seen one like it recently. Nothing came to me, so I pocketed it and picked up Mitzi. "I don't know how, but you keep digging up more clues for us. This earring could be important. Good girl." I'd return the piece to Noreen in the morning, so she could check to see if anyone had reported losing it.

Ben opened the front door and called out my name. "Abby, we're here, and we have some news."

Harry followed him in. "I just got a call from a friend of mine at the station, and he gave me the information about that number you gave me. It was a license plate number, and I'm going to look it up and let you know what I find."

I drummed my fingers on the counter by the coffee pot. "Well, well, Mrs. Wentworth is more observant than we give her credit for. First thing after breakfast I'll pay her another visit."

I poured the coffee into mugs on a tray and added a plate of muffins I had taken from the freezer. When I set them on the table, Ben grabbed a blueberry one.

"That's a good idea. She may remember something else. I've been thinking about the funeral, too. Let's check at breakfast to see who at our table plans or wants to go to Pete's service. We could all go in one of our cars and not take up space on the van."

It wouldn't be mine because it only holds five. Clara and Doris don't drive, and Bessie's was the same size as mine, so that left Ben or Harry to drive. "Which one of you wants the honor?"

Harry laughed and poked his chest with his thumb. "Me, of course, I'm the only one with a big enough car."

His SUV did seat seven, so we had our ride to the service, but now it was time to get back to other things.

I pulled the earring from my pocket. "Mitzi brought me this a while ago. Not sure where she found it, but I know I've seen it on someone around here before. It's not for pierced ears, so it could have easily fallen off any lady in our community."

Harry held out his hand, so I handed it to him. He eyed it from several angles. "I think I've see this, too. Do you plan to turn it in? It could be another clue in our mystery."

"Well, yes, I was going to give it to Noreen tomorrow, but the longer I look at it, I'm not sure any of the women who live here would wear one like that. It's a rather large stone and has an intricate designed frame around it. The color is unusual, too. Not really purple, but not maroon either. It also looks like it may be hand-crafted."

Ben shook his head. "I wouldn't know anything about that, but it will be interesting to see who has the matching one." He frowned with his eyebrows bunched together. "Why not post a notice on the bulletin board and see who answers it."

"A good idea, but I think I'll hang on to it a little longer."

"Okay. I'll make up a lost sign for it without a description then whoever says they lost one will have to describe it or show the other one. Whenever you decide, it'll be ready." Ben drank the last drops of his coffee. "It's getting late, so I'm heading home. How about you, Harry?"

"I'm right behind you."

I followed them to the door where Ben stopped. "Do you mind if I go with you to visit Olivia in the morning?"

"After giving it some thought, I think I'd rather do it alone. It'll be less confusing for her if no one is with me."

"You're probably right, but be sure to let us know what you find out. I'll go with Harry in the morning, and then we can meet here tomorrow afternoon."

"Of course I will let you know about Olivia. We're in this together. See you tomorrow afternoon." I started to close the door but remembered Bessie. "Oh, and Ben, be sure you apologize to Bessie in the morning for skipping out on your Bridge game tonight."

Ben's face colored. "I guess I should. I didn't give her any excuse or explanation. I don't know why I agreed to be her partner again except I like to win." He winked and backed off the porch.

"Well, you won't this time. Right, Harry?"

He grinned and gave me a thumbs-up sign. I shooed them off of the porch. "Now get on, both of you. I'll see you tomorrow."

I closed the door behind them. It was only a little after nine, so I decided to pop some corn and watch a Hallmark movie I'd taped earlier.

The movie was good, but my mind wandered off in all directions. The more I thought about it, the more I became convinced that earring had something to do with Pete's murder. If it was a clue and belonged to the killer, we'd be in trouble for withholding evidence. I couldn't say if it had actually been found at the scene, so I wasn't really hindering the police from their investigation.

The fact that Olivia had remembered the license plate number still amazed me, and it meant she may have seen a lot more than she told us before. I switched off the TV. I'd watch the movie some other time.

I made a list of questions and things I could say to Olivia to help her remember that day. I prayed she'd have more lucid moments and give us a clue that would lead us to a prime suspect. Harry could then turn the information over to that detective. If I did, and told him the source, he might not believe me, but he'd listen to Harry.

Tomorrow might turn out to be a most interesting day.

Chapter 11

After breakfast the next morning, I went in search of Noreen to see if she had returned to work.

Taryn stepped out of her office at the same time I arrived at her door. "Oh, Mrs. Billings, you're just the one I wanted to see."

"Oh, I came by to check on Noreen. Is she coming back to work today?"

"No, the doctor said one more day, so she'll be here tomorrow. Now, what I wanted to see you about. We have the food arranged and everything set for the Harvest Banquet. Our guest speaker is a Christian comic recommended by Reverend Lewis. You need to form a committee and get started on what we can use. We have a harvest theme, so you can go from that. Be sure to check with Mr. Kirk about the flowers as well."

"I can do that. Do you have any suggestions for the floral arrangements?" Something else to add to my list of "to-do," but I couldn't disappoint our residents.

"Some bronze and gold mums would be great and other fall flowers that might be available."

That wouldn't be so difficult. "I'll speak to Mr.

he woman?"

ink it was our Miss Burns.

woman came out there."

ther woman? Not Taryn

ghter hair than Taryn, but I
He sure was busy talking to
ng to his business. I'll have to
about this. Can't have our
so much time talking. Then the
my morning medication, and I
lse."

t into overdrive. Now we had
ering the scene. With binoculars
lent view of everything. Still, no
tioned a second person talking
was the man in the car?

gives you some interesting things
birds."

"Yes, it does. My memory is
tricks on me, but sometimes I
angest things."

a, did you recognize anything at all
you saw?'

't really see her that well even with
but she did have on pants and a short
k, and I'm sure I've seen her around

ust be one of the employees. Our list
kept growing.

od and hung the binoculars around
time for me to watch my birds. I'm
ntworth isn't here, but I'll tell him you

Kirk about it today." I started to ask why she couldn't speak to Tom Kirk herself, but she was taking over Noreen's duties as well, so I figured she must have a good reason. Then I remembered one of the reasons I wanted to see her or Noreen in the first place.

"By the way, I thought you'd like to know that Ben, Harry, and the others in our group are going to Pete's funeral in Harry's car. That should make for more room in the van."

"Great. Thanks for telling me. The van is filling up, and this will allow for more residents."

"I'm glad, now I must run some errands." I hurried away before she could think of some other task I could do for the dinner. Not that I minded helping, but I had too many other things on my mind, the first being my visit with Olivia Wentworth.

I knocked on Olivia's door, and a strange woman opened it. "Hello, I'm Abigail Billings, and I live in one of the cottages. Is Mrs. Wentworth available for a visit?"

A grin spread across her face. "Oh, Mrs. Billings, Mother has mentioned you. I'm Georgene Wentworth, Olivia's daughter-in-law. Please, come in."

I did, but with a little apprehension. How much would I be able to get from Olivia with Georgene here?

"Olivia will be out in a moment. May I get you a cup of tea or coffee? We just finished breakfast, so the coffee is hot and fresh."

"Coffee would be nice, Mrs. Wentworth."

"Oh, do please call me Georgene. I feel like I know you from all I've heard about how you solved the mystery of the missing money and the embezzling a few months ago."

Heat rose up my neck. Of course, she'd know about that since she was the wife of the board president. "I'm glad I was able to help Spring Hills police catch the thief."

"Trenton was as well." She set a mug of coffee on the table. "Here comes Olivia now."

I'd never seen the woman when she didn't look like she was ready for guests, and this morning was no exception. Her white hair held a perfect coif, and her face glowed with subtle make-up. Even her attire, navy wool slacks and a blue sweater fit her slight frame to perfection.

"Mother, Mrs. Billings has dropped by to see you." She pulled out a chair for Olivia to be seated across from Abigail.

Olivia smiled and leaned forward. "Where's that handsome man you were with the other day?"

My goodness, she remembered our visit. "He's off taking care of some business. I'll tell him you asked about him."

"Please do, and Georgene, I'd like another cup of coffee please."

Georgene headed for the kitchen and the coffee pot. She returned a moment later and set the cup and saucer before Olivia.

"Thank you, dear. Now, Abigail, are you here again about that awful murder?"

I jerked back. Wow, I hadn't expected that. "In a way, but I wanted to thank you for the numbers

came by to visit. What was your name again?"

I glanced at Georgene. She shrugged and shook her head.

"Her memory lapses are becoming much more frequent. When she's lucid and in the present, she sees and hears a lot, but then, without much warning, she retreats to the past.

I reached for Olivia's hand. "Just tell him Mrs. Billings came by."

She squeezed my hand in hers. "Do come back for a visit." She dropped my hand, turned, and headed for the windows.

At least she still remembered what she was going to do.

"It's time for me to leave. She's been helpful with what she remembers and is a delightful person. I'm so sorry for her condition."

"It's been difficult because she was always so active in charitable affairs and entertaining her husband's business associates. I'm glad she was able to give you information this morning. Do come again because she enjoys having visitors. I try to get by at least once a week."

That was strange. This was the first time I'd ever seen her here, but then I couldn't know *all* of what went on around Spring Hills.

I said my goodbyes and left. Olivia may not be much for an eyewitness in court, but I had the facts she'd given me when she knew who I was. Ben would certainly be surprised to learn about the binoculars.

I hurried out to my house to write everything down before heading over to see Mr. Kirk about the flowers for the dinner. While I enjoyed another cup of coffee and a few chocolate chip cookies, I went over our notes.

We had Maria, the second woman, Taryn Burns, Adam and Steve all having arguments with Steve. Then there was the man in car. He could have done it and gotten away. Steve was supposed to be on vacation this week, but he could have come that morning, killed Pete and disappeared with a good alibi. We'd have to find out if Steve had really been out of town that particular morning.

I had a lot to tell Ben and Harry soon as I could find them. They were going on some errands this morning, so I most likely wouldn't see them until after lunch.

I spent the next few hours going over all the information we'd gleaned so far. I had Taryn and Maria arguing with Pete as well as another woman after Taryn. Adam and Steve had argued with him as well, so that made at least five people who had disagreements with our gardener.

Adam deserved a second visit. Whatever he was hiding, I wanted to know. I had my regular tee time schedule, so I could see him then. I also had to check and find out if Steve really was on vacation and out of town. If not, I would add him to the list of prime suspects.

I put away my lists and prepared a quick lunch. I wanted to get over to Tom Kirk's office and take care of the flowers before finding Ben and Harry. I closed Mitzi up in the bathroom and headed for Mr. Kirk's office.

The grounds manager greeted me with a

hearty hello and a handshake. "How can I help you today?"

"Taryn said Pete always ordered the flowers for the Harvest dinner, but since he's no longer with us, will you be able to take care of them?"

"Of course, I'd be happy to. I know the florist he used, so I'll use the same one. What did you have in mind?"

"Our color scheme will need mums and other flowers in the yellow, gold, and bronze range. Taryn plans on decorating every table in the dining hall with a small arrangement. I thought flowers along with gourds and small pumpkins or cornucopias I'm going to buy would look nice. The tablecloths will be yellow-gold and brown."

As I talked he wrote on a pad. "I think we can get that done with no problems. I'll check with Miss Burns about the delivery time and set-up."

"Thank you, so much. I have a group of friends who will help with all the decorating." I started to ask him a few more questions about Pete but the phone rang. He excused himself saying it was business he had to take care of, so I left.

Back at the main building, I found Taryn and gave her the information about the flowers.

"I knew you'd come through for me. Your ideas are always so good. The decorations will be lovely, and I'm glad a few of the ladies will help you decorate." She handed me an envelope. "Here is your money for supplies. Get whatever you need."

I thanked her, and we parted ways. Getting the flowers had been too easy and made me a little suspicious of Taryn's explanation earlier. Maybe the argument was about something else. I'd have to mull that over for a while.

Since I had no idea what time Ben and Harry would be back, this would be a good time do a little sleuthing myself and check again with Adam.

When I walked past the kitchen counter, I spotted the earring Mitzi had found. I'd almost forgotten about it with my visit to Olivia. I still hadn't remembered exactly where I had seen it or who was wearing it.

Maybe it would come to me later, but now it was time to get some more answers.

Chapter 12

I headed down to the golf shop to speak with Adam. My usual tee off time is around two, but I decided it might have to be canceled for today depending on what time Harry and Ben returned.

Adam's eyebrows arched when he saw me. "Mrs. Billings, I didn't see your name on the schedule for a tee time this morning. I have you at our usual slot. Did I miss something?"

"No, you didn't miss anything. I have a few questions for you about Pete."

A veil ascended over his eyes. "Pete? Whatever for?"

Since I wasn't sure exactly where to start, I just plunged ahead. "Doris Barton said she saw you and Pete arguing one day last week. Could you tell me what that was all about?"

The tips of his ears reddened like a tomato ripening in the sun. "Oh, that. It was just about the greens needing closer mowing."

"Hmm. Mrs. Barton said you were really angry with Pete and said something about his owing you and you wanted your share. In fact, she said it looked like you were going to hit Pete."

His swallowed hard. "I guess I can be honest

with you. Mrs. Barton doesn't miss anything. Yes, I was mad at him because he didn't bring some money he owed me that day like he'd promised. Steve, Pete, and I won a bunch of money in one of those Oklahoma casinos. Pete was going to invest it for us, but then I decided I wanted mine back, but it was too late, he'd already put it in some stocks or something, but he still said he'd have my part for me."

"But you say he was going to bring it to you that day."

"Yeah, but he wanted to give Maria some money to help pay for her little girl's expenses. Then I found out later they argued about it, and she wouldn't even take it. Then before he had a chance to pay up, someone did him in."

"I see. How will you get your money now?"

He shook his head. "Honestly, Mrs. Billings, I don't know. Pete invested the winnings in some account, but I never did get a chance to find out where or what. Guess that was kind of stupid. I have to wait until Steve gets back, and he's going to be mighty upset when he learns about all of this."

Not exactly stupid, but not very smart either. Mentally I crossed him off our suspect list because he had more of a motive to keep Pete alive than to kill him. "I'm surprised someone hasn't told him, so he could come back here for the funeral."

"He can't. He's on a cruise with his family to celebrate his parents' anniversary. He didn't say which line or where they were going. Oh, man, this will tear him up. He and Pete were really good buddies."

"Thanks, Adam. I'll see you at my regular time." I decided not to cancel my game for this afternoon. The guys could wait for me to finish my normal schedule. Wouldn't hurt Ben to join me, but that wasn't likely to happen.

I glanced at my watch. The visits with Olivia and Adam had taken less than two hours, so I had some time before lunch. My regular habits and errands had been sadly neglected this past week, so I climbed into my car and headed for the shopping center. Mitzi needed food, and so did I. The worries of the past week had certainly depleted my supply.

I made a stop by the craft store to check out anything that would be good for the dinner decorations. Taryn had ordered napkins and tablecloths from a linen supply, so what I purchased had to match those. I found some clever party favors in the shape of cornucopias as well as bales of hay, miniature pumpkins, some pilgrim figures, and Indians. When I checked out, the items totaled up a little less than the amount Taryn had given me, and I was quite proud of myself. I hadn't stayed within a budget for more years than I cared to remember.

After buying my groceries, I stopped by the pet center. Mitzi needed a carrier, so she wouldn't be locked up in the bathroom or my bedroom all the time. After buying one that would give her plenty of room, I headed back home. The errands had taken longer than I planned, so I stopped and grabbed lunch to go.

When I arrived home, Ben met me in the driveway. "Where have you been? I've been waiting all morning for you to show up."

"My stars, Ben, I do have a life you know."

"I'm sorry." He reached for a bag. "Here, let me help with these." He laughed when he spotted the carrier. "You think Mitzi's going to stay in that thing?"

"Of course, she will. She's a good baby. Leave it and I'll get it later."

He closed the trunk lid and followed me inside. Mitzi jumped all around our feet. I'm used to her otherwise I would have tripped like Ben did. He stumbled against the cabinet, and Mitzi let out a yelp and scurried for the safety of the other room.

"Good thing I like that little fur ball so much, but I'm glad she's yours and not mine."

Mitzi's anything but a fur ball, but she could get in the way with her curiosity.

Harry stuck his head through a crack in the patio door. "Hey, glad you're back, Abby. Ben and I have some news."

"Okay, so what have you learned?" I filled the coffee pot while the men sat at the table.

Harry sat back in his chair with a wide grin on his face and pulled a piece of paper from his pocket. "That license plate number is registered to a Lenny Fields."

"Who is he, and what was he doing in my driveway?"

"That's the interesting part. He's connected to a group in this area that has those poker games."

I studied Harry's face. "Have you said anything to the police yet about this Fields guy?"

"No, but I did get his address, and Ben and I

will check him out later. Now, what did you learn from Olivia?"

After I relayed what I had discovered, Ben and Harry shook their heads in disbelief. Ben let out a low whistle.

"Binoculars? I never would have guessed that." Then he chuckled. "Never knew a guy with so many people angry with him at one time. Adam, Taryn and Maria have admitted their arguments, and according to Tillie, he had one with Steve, but who is this other woman Olivia claims to have seen?"

We pondered that for a few moments, but none of us came up with a name. I tapped my fingers on the table. "If he had another woman he'd been dating, he could have been caught in a love triangle."

Ben nodded and pursed his lips. "That's an avenue worth exploring with what we've learned so far about his love interests."

I shoved back from the table. "Well, I don't have time for that now. I have a tee time in fifteen minutes, and I don't want to be late. "Before you leave, will you bring in the kennel from my car? I'm going to try it out with Mitzi while I play."

When he and Harry both went outside, I glanced at the paper Harry had on the table. There was Lenny Field's address. I copied it onto a note pad of my own and stowed it in the drawer at the same time the two of them came in the back door.

"Thanks, you can put it in the hallway for now."

After placing Mitzi in her crate, Ben looked at me with narrowed eyes. "I think I might join you on the course. I'll stop by my place and get my other jacket and meet you there."

My mouth dropped open. Ben was actually going to do something requiring exercise?

"Don't act so surprised. You've asked me enough times, and today is a beautiful day, so I'll see you there."

Before I could respond, he was gone with Harry following and shaking his head.

When I arrived at the golf shop, Ben was arguing with Adam.

"Sorry, Mr. Martin, but we can't let you have a cart without a doctor's letter saying you can't walk at least nine holes."

Ben sighed. "Believe me I'll have trouble walking the distance today."

I'd heard enough. "If you can't walk the course, you shouldn't even come."

"Come on, Abby, we need to talk some more. Adam here understands."

Adam handed Ben the keys. "I'll do it this time, but you really should be walking."

I followed him to the carts. "Ben Martin! What do you think you're doing?"

"Going to watch you play golf and learn how. I don't even have any clubs right now."

"You'll do no such thing. Golf is a walking game around here, so you can walk and learn."

"I either ride, or I don't go at all." Ben gripped the steering wheel of the cart.

There was no arguing with him, but I intended to get in my game. "Whatever, but do you know how to drive that thing?"

"How difficult can it be? I've driven a car for forever. Now show me what you can do."

I headed for the first tee with Ben following me. A few seconds later, my shot sent the ball sailing down the fairway. I marched off in the direction it landed.

"Hey, am I going to ride by myself?" Ben shouted and stepped on the accelerator.

He followed along and stayed in the cart until the seventh hole. Then he climbed from the cart and stood with his arms crossed over his chest. "Golf is a pointless sport. What kind of fun is it to hit a little ball then chase it down and hit it again? What's the point?"

I glared at him before I swung and sent the ball down the fairway. With him following like this, nine holes would the limit for today.

He climbed back into the cart to head for the next tee. When he stepped on the accelerator, the car jumped ahead like a stone out of slingshot and sped off across the fairway.

Ben yelled "Fore" and kept going.

I took off after him, leaving my clubs at the seventh tee. A foursome at the next tee jumped to clear a path for the errant vehicle. It looked like Ben stomped on the brake pedal but nothing happened.

His speed wasn't that much, but the back part of the course heading to the golf shop was downhill, so the cart picked up speed.

I watched the cart bump and jump over the rise and on down a fairway. It ran through a sand trap with Ben yelling all the way. The cart didn't stop, but splashed through the water hazard on the ninth hole.

The cart kept running with Ben hanging on for dear life. Several golfers tried to chase him down. I cringed when I realized he was headed straight for the hedge separating the last putting green from the sidewalk. Ben curled up into a ball and made a dive off of the cart. He rolled a few feet and landed on his back.

I raced up to him as did several other golfers. "Are you okay? Can you move?"

He tried to sit up, but grimaced in pain, so I helped just as Adam arrived.

"Here, let me get him. He's too heavy for you."

I stepped back and let Adam help Ben to his feet. Ben scowled. "That crazy machine tried to kill me."

Matt shook his head. "No, Sir. You just jammed the accelerator pedal. I'll take it back to the shack." He turned to Abby. "Think you can get him up to his cottage alone?"

"I'll help her." Harry appeared at Ben's side, and he couldn't contain his laughter. "I was coming back from the tennis courts when I heard the commotion over here. That was quite a ride Ben old boy."

Ben's face flushed a deep red, and he jerked away from Harry. "I don't need your help, and I don't need a doctor. I'll be fine."

After a few steps, he stopped. "Well, maybe I'll go up and get doc to look at it and put an ice pack on my ankle and shoulder."

I glanced at Harry who was still grinning, and then turned to scold Ben. "That was the dumbest thing I've ever seen. You shouldn't have been trying to drive that thing. When will you ever learn just to do what you're supposed to do?"

Ben glowered at me, but he continued on to the clinic. Harry caught up with him and he didn't complain about Harry's help. An hour later we emerged with a sling supporting his arm. It had been a simple shoulder sprain, but bad enough for him to not use his left arm for a while.

I walked beside him. "I'm sorry for your pain, but it was your fault."

The scowl he gave me said more than the words he didn't say. One thing for certain, this day certainly wasn't going like I'd planned.

Chapter 13

After Ben's accident, nothing more was said or done about Pete's murder. Ben had gone back to his place with his pain pills, and Harry said he'd wait until Ben felt better to go see Lenny.

On Tuesday, the day of the funeral, the breakfast table buzzed with Ben's accident. The other women had to know all about it. I had the errant earring in my pocket to give to Noreen who was supposed to be back today, so I ate quickly.

I left them all still talking about poor Ben. Knowing him, he'd milk that sore shoulder for all it was worth.

Noreen's door was ajar, so I knocked and entered. "Good morning, Noreen, we're glad you're feeling better and back on the job."

"Thanks, Abigail. It's good to be back. How can I help you this morning?" She shuffled some papers on her desk and slid them into a folder.

When she glanced up at me, my heart did a double take. She wore earrings exactly like the one I'd found except a different color.

"Those are beautiful earrings you have on. May I ask where you got them?"

"At the War Eagle fair. I bought them last year. A jewelry craftsman makes them and sells them there. They're really popular."

The one I had burned in my pocket, but I wasn't sure I wanted to give it to Noreen just yet. "I've noticed fewer lost and found items listed on the bulletin board. Are we not having as many losses as we once did?"

Noreen shrugged and laughed. "Not sure. Either they're getting more careful or just not turning in what they find. I don't get many reports of lost items either."

"Let's hope it's because they're more careful." I wanted to get back to the topic of that earring.

"Is the War Eagle fair the only place you can get the earrings?"

"I think this particular one is, but the crafts people exhibits aren't exclusive to the fair. They go other places during the year, but I've never seen this particular craftsman anywhere but War Eagle."

"That's too bad. I'd like to purchase some jewelry like that."

"I'll check with you the next time I plan to go and maybe pick up a piece or two for you."

"I would like that, thanks." If I didn't figure out to whom the one I had belonged, I'd give it to her, but I wanted to a little more detective work before that.

I left her office and stopped by Carrie's desk. "Will any of the staff be attending the funeral service for Pete this afternoon?"

"Taryn reserved the big van for any of the residents who wanted to go. It filled up quickly."

"I'm not surprised. Pete was well liked. How about you?"

Her eyes opened wide. "What about me?"

"Are you going to the funeral?"

Red flooded her face, but her shoulders relaxed. She picked up a stack of papers and flipped through them. "No. I can't leave. Someone has to stay and be in charge."

"Oh, I'm sorry." I left and headed home. Something about Carrie skittered around in my head, but I had other things to do now.

The main dining hall doors were closed, and everyone had left. I didn't see Ben or Harry, so I went on to my cottage. I glanced at Carrie's when I made my way back outside. Her behavior niggled at the edge of my mind. Something seemed out of kilter, but I couldn't quite get it into focus. Every time I mentioned Pete, she reacted differently. I'd have to mention that to Ben, too. One of the people I'd talked to had said Carrie was one of Pete's girlfriends, so I guess that accounted for her strange behavior. Mercy, that man was gigolo despite how nice everyone thought he was.

I decided to wait until after the funeral to talk with Ben. He needed to rest as much as possible since we'd be out most of the afternoon. His accident on the golf course had ended up with an injury, but I couldn't help but laugh at the memory of him hanging on to the cart as it careened down the fairway and into that hedge. Maybe that little mishap would teach him a lesson about the benefits of walking.

I spent the rest of the morning taking care of

chores around my house. I had sorely neglected it for close to a week. After a quick lunch I dressed for Pete's funeral service. Promptly at one-thirty, Harry drove up in his SUV. He had picked up Ben, Bessie and Clara first. Ben sat in front with Harry because of his shoulder. I joined Bessie and Clara on the middle seat. Harry said Doris wasn't feeling well and decided not to attend.

I didn't talk much on ten-minute drive to the service. I had been surprised when told the services would be at a local church instead of the funeral home, but I learned his family was active at this church. Made me want to know why he had taken up gambling and women.

The Spring Hills van sat parked in a space for the handicapped when we arrived. It held fifteen people, and I was a bit curious to see who had come.

We entered the sanctuary, and many people already filled the pews. Ben led us to a row behind the Spring Hills group. Taryn must have driven the van. Jim Tate, Tillie, Reverend Lewis, Nell Clark and several others whose names I didn't know were there along with the Stewarts and Clays who must have driven their own cars. More people than I realized cared about Pete.

I read the handout given us when we signed the book in the foyer and the information there was quite interesting. Pete served his country then returned to work at Spring Hills while attending college to study landscape design. No wonder that boy knew so much about plants and taking care of them. Now I wished I had made the effort to know him better. But that gambling bit still bothered me.

The sheet listed the members of his family, two sisters and three brothers and his parents. We stood as they all filed in to sit in the reserved section in the front. All his siblings had families because it took more than a few rows to seat them all. After a prayer, we stood and sang *It Is Well With My Soul*. I love that song. It had been sung at more than a few services I had attended in the past and would be at mine as well.

All during the eulogy and remembrances, I noticed Ben wore a rather bored look. That gave me something to think about. Come to think of it, Ben rarely attended our Sunday evening services, but I'd figured he'd been to church in the morning so didn't feel the need to come again. Maybe not. I tucked that into the back of mind for more exploration later.

A glance around the room revealed more people from Spring Hills had attended. Mr. Kirk was in attendance as well as several other members of the grounds crew who must have come in their own cars. In fact, the church was filled to capacity from what I could see. What a nice thing for his mother to have for a memory.

Ben yawned and a few minutes later his eyes closed. I nudged him with my elbow, and he shot me a look that told me not to do that again. I wouldn't, but I didn't understand his behavior.

After the service we waited outside until the hearse left the premises with its entourage of cars before heading back to Harry's car. The first few minutes were quiet, but Bessie didn't take long to start a conversation.

"Now that was a lovely service. He certainly came from a large family."

"Yes, he did. The pastor did a wonderful job with his message. So much hope for the family." I glanced at Ben while I spoke, but he simply worked his mouth in a way men do when they are displeased or trying to keep from saying something they shouldn't.

Bessie and Clara kept up the conversation, but I kept my eye on Ben in the front passenger seat. After dinner, we needed to have a little talk.

Bessie mentioned the Harvest Dinner and gave me my opening to join in. "I want to thank all of you for volunteering to help me decorate. I bought some decorations yesterday for us to use on the tables. Mr. Kirk is getting the floral arrangements for us."

Bessie's eyes lit up like a neon sign on Broadway. That lady loved a party of any kind. Even Clara's eyes reflected her excitement.

Ben grunted. "What next? Are you going to sign us up for the ballroom dancing lessons?"

Harry laughed. "Oh, come on, sport. This will be fun."

"As long as I don't have to do a lot of work using my shoulder, I guess I can help." He rubbed his sling to emphasize his point.

I might have known that the others had to put in their two cents worth, but Ben didn't respond. His woeful expression told me all I needed to know about his bid for sympathy.

After we arrived back at Spring Hills, Harry

dropped everyone off. Ben followed me to my cottage and Harry joined us after he parked his car.

I told them about my visit with Mr. Kirk. "You know, Taryn told me she and Pete argued over the flowers because he didn't want to get involved, but from the way Kirk talked, Pete enjoyed doing that, and I can see why he would if he was taking classes in landscaping. Doesn't make sense for him to argue with Taryn about it if he liked doing it."

Ben drummed his fingers on the table. "No it doesn't. I think you need to question Taryn Burns a little further.

I thought so too and would do that soon. "When are you going to check out this Lenny person?"

Harry shrugged. "Soon as I can get around to it. Thought I'd talk to him before giving the number to the police."

"You don't think they'll be upset for not turning it in sooner?"

"No, I'll explain the car was parked near yours, and you wanted it checked out."

That sounded plausible, but I sure didn't want them thinking we were withholding evidence.

Ben's bushy white eyebrows knit together. "I still can't believe Olivia actually uses binoculars to watch birds every morning. Why, she probably knows more about what goes on around here than anybody, including Tillie."

"Yes, and it's all locked in her mind, and I'm afraid the key won't be working too well in the future. The whole thing saddens me after listening to her daughter-in-law talk about how active Olivia was before her memory problems."

Harry sipped his coffee. "Alzheimer's is a terrible disease. My brother's wife is in a memory care facility down in Little Rock. It's been difficult watching the changes in her. She doesn't know any of us now." He shook his head as if to clear it. "Let's talk about something else."

This was as good a time as any to tell them about my conversation with Noreen this morning, but for some reason, I withheld that information, and stayed quiet.

Ben rubbed his chin. "Sure would be nice to know who that last woman he argued with is. She has to be from around here."

I thought so as well, but until we had a better description, she'd remain the mystery woman.

Chapter 14

Since we'd exhausted any new information, Ben and Harry left. Ben didn't look happy at all, but he followed Harry out the door. It was still late afternoon with a little over two hours until dinner, and I wanted to get more information. I remembered the address for Lenny and found the note I had written. A quick look at a map on my computer, and I had the information I needed to find this Lenny Fields.

Fifteen minutes later I drove down the street I had written down. Now that I was here, my doubts surfaced. What made me think I could talk to and question someone mixed up in illegal gambling? Especially if he was a hit man or a collection goon or whatever they call the ones who do the dirty work. Besides that, he may not even be home this time of day. At the moment, I hoped he wasn't.

I drove into the apartment complex and immediately spotted the gray car. I checked the license plate and it was the same numbers as the ones Olivia had given us. *Abigail Billings, what are you doing here? You can't just walk up and confront this man.*

Why hadn't I waited for Ben and Harry and

come with them? Because they wouldn't have let me come, that's why.

The apartment numbers gleamed in the sun on the side of the building where Lenny lived. I parked the car and sat there a few moments to gather up my courage. A door opened and a man stepped outside. He fit the description Olivia had given, brief as it was. When he beeped his remote and the lights of the gray car came on, I knew it was Lenny.

Before I could think about what I would do, I jumped from the car and ran over. I figured I'd be safe outdoors in the open. "Lenny Fields?"

He turned toward me and eyed me like I had two heads or something. "Who wants to know?"

"My name is Abby Billings, and I live in the complex where Pete Simpson was killed."

A veil dropped over his eyes as they narrowed. "And what does that have to do with me?"

"Well, I was wondering why you were parked in my driveway by my white car?" I pointed in the direction where my car sat. "I saw the car around the time Pete was killed. I wondered what the car was doing in my drive and thought you might have seen something." I prayed forgiveness for my little white lie.

He blew out his breath then shrugged. "Look, lady, I don't know nothing about this Pete guy and his murder."

I knew that wasn't the truth. "Then why were you there? And you can't deny you were."

He seemed to ponder this a moment. "You sure you're not with the police?"

I planted my hands on my hips. "Do I look like

I'm from the police?"

"Umm…no, but you sure are nosy."

I pulled myself up straighter and lifted my head. "See here, I'm not being nosy. I just want some answers."

Suddenly he laughed. I didn't see anything funny at all, but apparently, he must have.

"What did you say your name was again?"

"Abigail Billings."

"All right, Abigail Billings, I'll tell you what happened." He leaned against his car and crossed his arms over his chest. "I did go there to see Pete that day. I saw him mowing the lawn but decided to wait until he was closer to my car. When I got out, a woman stopped him and they had an argument about something. Looked like Pete won because the lady stomped off like a bull ready to charge."

That must have been Taryn. She had a few more questions to answer about that argument.

Lenny continued. "Pete started working in the flower bed there by a house, and again I started toward him. But another woman came running from the main building and confronted him. This time the argument really got loud. I heard her tell him to leave Maria alone because she wasn't his type."

His explanation fit with the second woman, but who was she and why did she mention Maria?"

"What did this second woman look like?"

"Well, she was pretty. She had brownish hair, and she wasn't as tall as the first one."

"What was she wearing, and was she young or old?"

"I didn't pay any attention to what she had on. I

was more interested in what she was doing, but she didn't have on a coat, and her clothes were dark. I'd say she was about the same age as Pete."

His description didn't help much with identifying our mystery woman, but she had come from the main building and was young.

Lenny straightened up. "I saw what happened next. This gal picked up a rock and banged Pete on the back of the head with it. When he fell, she just looked at the rock then ran off with it in her hands. That's when I hightailed it outta there. I wouldn't be collecting any money from Pete."

Oh my. Now that mystery woman became the prime suspect in my book. If what he told me had any truth in it, the second woman killed Pete. But she hit him with the rock. Had that been enough to kill him? And how did the aerator get into his stomach?

"I wonder why she ran away with the rock instead of dropping it." Dumb question to ask if the rock had killed Pete, she wouldn't leave it for evidence.

"Probably because it had blood on it." He jangled his keys in my face. "If you'll excuse me, lady, I have work to do."

"Oh, of course, thank you for telling me this. Would you be willing to tell the police what you saw?"

He looked at me like I'd lost my marbles. "Lady, I'm not talking to the police about anything, and if I were you, I wouldn't get involved. No telling what may happen to you."

I squared my shoulders and scowled. "Are you

threatening me, Lenny Fields?"

"No, ma'am, just stating facts. No need for you to get mixed up in Pete's mess."

He opened his car door and leaned on it. "If the police happen around, I'll deny any knowledge of what I saw. So, watch what you say, Mrs. Billings." He climbed into his car then drove off.

I didn't like that one bit, but he wasn't going to intimidate me. And now at least I had another clue. The second woman had to be found.

I rushed back to the center, but phoned Ben on the way, and he wanted to know where I was. I told him to get Harry and meet me back at my place. Sure enough, both men waited for me in the carport. Soon as I exited my car, Ben grabbed my arm with his good right hand.

"Where in tarnation have you been? I thought you were taking a nap and resting like the rest of us."

I shoved his hand away and marched into the house. "I don't need daytime naps, and I was curious about something."

Harry groaned. "Oh no, don't tell me. You went to find Lenny Fields."

They followed me to the kitchen with Ben and Harry both fussing all the way. I could have been hurt, or kidnapped, or killed.

"Guys, shut your mouths. I'm fine. None of those things happened, but I did get some interesting news. If you'll sit quietly for a few minutes, I'll tell you.

Both men settled down, but from the looks on their faces, they weren't happy about it.

After I finished my tale, Harry shook his head. "There's our killer. Pete fell forward and that's when the aerator stuck in his stomach. Since he was most likely unconscious or dazed from the blow on the head, he couldn't get off the aerator or get it out of his stomach. I bet the coroner's report shows he bled to death."

Ben slapped his hand on the table. "That's it. Whoever hit him didn't intentionally kill him, but the result was the same. If she'd come forward and admit what happened, she most likely wouldn't be charged with first degree murder."

I reached into the drawer for my pad and pen.

Harry leaned on the counter with his forearms. "You may be right, but we still don't know who the woman is. I'll have to give the police the license plate number now."

"Okay, but look at our list. We can eliminate Steve and Adam since Lenny didn't see a man out there with Pete. I still can't believe all this went on while we were having breakfast. Just seems weird."

Ben tapped his fingers on the counter. "But it did, so now we have to figure out who this woman is. We know of two who admit arguing with him and one who went outside. Maria stayed in the building looking for her keys and going about her work. Taryn argued about flowers and went outside to confront him. The mystery woman came from the main building, so it could have been Taryn returning or Noreen, or Carrie, or any of the housekeeping staff."

This was doing no good. "We have to keep digging. You two take care of the police, and I'll do some more nosing around here. Taryn's story about the flowers doesn't ring true. Lenny's description of the argument sounded much too intense to be over flowers for a dinner."

"You're right." Ben glanced at his watch. "It's supper time. You may have to wait until tomorrow to question Taryn again."

That was all right with me. I'd had enough today to last a few days, but I'd be on it tomorrow. I stowed my pen and pad back in the drawer and retrieved my jacket from the closet.

"Y'all go on, and I'll catch up to you. I want to let Mitzi out for a few minutes."

The two men left for their own cottages, and I opened the carrier to let Mitzi out. She yipped at me like I'd put her in prison. "Sorry, sweet girl, but you have to get used to it. C'mon and we'll go outside for a few minutes.

While Mitzi ran around the yard then took care of business, I had to come up with a tactful way to ask Taryn about that argument and if she'd seen anyone else come out to see Pete.

After I took care of Mitzi, I headed up to the main building for supper. When I crossed the hallway, I paused and looked down toward the bulletin board. On a whim, I strolled down to it to check to see if anyone listed an earring like the one I had as being lost. I searched and searched, but it was nowhere on the board.

Then I thought of Noreen again. Maybe it had been her after all. She had brown hair, and from a distance one couldn't see the gray strands there. I didn't recall what she had been wearing that day, but then I wasn't thinking about her as a suspect and didn't notice her clothes.

I sighed and headed back to the dining area. One more name to add to my list of people to question.

Chapter 15

The next morning after breakfast, I headed for Noreen's office. She waved me in and closed the door.

"What can I do for you this morning? Are you having any problems with the dinner and decorations?"

"No, we have that all under control. I was just curious about those earrings. I liked the one you had on yesterday. Do they come in different colors?"

"Yes, and he makes bracelets and necklaces to match, but they're expensive, so I stick to earrings. Since I don't have pierced ears, it's hard to find the clip-on type, so when I do, I buy several."

"I know what you mean because I do the same. I'd like to know when he might be having a show around here, so I can take a look at his jewelry." I really did want to check into seeing the jewelry, and it would give a good excuse to go into town.

"Of course, I'd be glad to let you know when he'll be back at War Eagle." She reached for the folder again.

Before she could speak, I asked, "Did you know two others besides Maria argued with Pete that morning?"

Her eyebrows rose and wrinkled her brow as she stared at me a moment. "Yes, but how did you know? That police detective told me when he came in to question me and Taryn again. Taryn admitted to her argument, and that makes her a suspect. Being honest about it may be in her favor."

I wanted to ask her about her dealings with Pete, but I didn't want to arouse any suspicions.

"You have your clues, so work your magic with them. I know you were told to stay out of it, but I have a feeling that's not going to stop you." She walked around her desk and opened the door for me to leave.

I stepped into the hall, frustration lacing my thoughts. I wish I had that much confidence in my abilities.

Taryn was by the bulletin board putting up a notice about the fall dinner.

"Hi, Taryn, I've been hearing good things from people about the dinner. It'll be good to get their minds off Pete's death."

"Oh, Abigail, good morning. Yes, I think they'll enjoy it, and I appreciate your help with the decorations." She pressed in the final thumb-tack. "We'll have a list of the nominees for Harvest King and Queen tonight at dinner."

A light exploded in my brain. Taryn could have easily gone back outside and argued with Pete again. Maybe she'd been up to War Eagle. None of our residents would have gone without a group or a family member took them. I might as well start my investigation now with the clock ticking.

"Taryn, what do you think about a field trip for

some of our more able-bodied residents. I've wanted to go to the craft fair at War Eagle, and some of the others might enjoy it as well."

"That's a great idea. I've never been myself and would love the opportunity to take some of you. Noreen told me they have some great booths. I'll have to think about that and come up with a plan. We could take the van, but we'll have to limit the number of people to fifteen with our driver. Let me check it out and get back with you."

The enthusiasm in her voice led me to believe she hadn't been there before, and if that was the case, she couldn't be the owner of that earring. Since I didn't know if the earring was a real clue, I didn't take Taryn off of my list. "I look forward to seeing what you can plan."

I left her taking care of the bulletin board and headed for the foyer. Steve waved at me and hurried over. "Mrs. Billings, I've just returned from vacation and learned about Pete. It's awful what happened to him. Do you have a few minutes to talk?"

Of course, I did. This was one young man I'd been itching to see all week. "Sure, let's go to the conference room. We can talk in private there.'

We headed in that direction. "I understand that you and Mr. Martin are doing a little bit of side investigating on your own, and I want to help."

He may have been back only today, but he already knew about what was going on. "How did you know about that?"

"Tillie. You know how she loves to tell all she knows about what's going on around here. I saw her when I went on duty a little before breakfast."

That explained a lot. We entered the library which was empty as it usually is this time of morning. We sat in a corner near a window. I wanted to get my questions in first, so I started with the one that had been on my mind the most. "Now, what can you tell me about your argument with Pete before you left?"

The startled expression on his face sure told the tale of being caught off-guard, which is exactly what I wanted.

He stared at his shoes or the floor or whatever, but he didn't look at me. Finally, he raised his head. "We had several disagreements before I left. One was because of Maria. He knew she was struggling to meet some medical bills for her daughter, and he wanted to help her out. She wanted no part of that, and I can't say that I blame her. Anyway, I told him to forget it and take care of other things first, but he went ahead and offered anyway."

Well, at least his story matched what Maria had said. "Was there something to do with the money you had won at the casinos?"

This time he shook his head. "I told Pete to keep his mouth shut. He doesn't realize how people around here listen when it appears they're doing something else."

He had that right by evidence of what I had learned. Maybe Harry ought to put out that little tidbit to his police buddies. Maybe then they could get this case solved, and I could get on with my business. Who was I kidding? I wanted to solve this crime myself, well with the help of Ben and Harry of course.

Steve continued with his information. "We invested the money we had won at the casinos, and don't ask how we won so much. That was Pete's doing. He lost some of his at the poker tables, but he accused them of cheating and didn't want to pay his debt."

"Do you have any idea who those people were?" That matched with what I had learned from Lenny.

"No, and I don't want to know. I don't play poker, so I never went with Pete."

I wasn't learning anything really new and nothing about who that second woman might be, but I had to keep prying.

"What about Pete and Adam? What was their relationship?"

"That was all over some money he gave Pete to invest for him. Adam didn't think it was growing fast enough and demanded his portion back. The money we won is in a joint account, so I'll talk with Adam and make sure he at least gets back what he invested."

"You know Pete better than the rest of us, so what can you tell me about the women in his life? Seems he had quite a few."

Steve laughed and shook his head. "Taryn told me you were investigating Pete's murder, but I had no idea you already knew so much about Pete. Until he became involved with Maria, he dated a lot without any commitments. He was falling in love with Maria and little Gracie, her daughter, but Maria wanted to take things slower."

"Who else was there besides Taryn and Maria?" This might borderline on gossip, but I had to find out who that mystery woman was.

This time he chuckled and blew out his breath. "You are determined aren't you?"

"We just want to get this whole thing cleared up. Some of our residents are still uneasy about Pete's death and are afraid the killer is still lurking about." I didn't actually know that for certain about any of the residents but Bessie, and she had let it be known she was being cautious."

"I think he was involved with several of the single maids and one of the nurses as well, and maybe even Carrie. One time he mentioned one of the wait staff in the dining hall. I quit listening to all that. As long as it didn't hurt our game, I didn't pay much attention to his dating life."

The mention of Carrie really perked my ears. She'd been upset by his death, but so had everyone else. Something I was missing kept darting around the edges of my thoughts. Carrie had been more distracted than usual since Pete's death, and she did have brown hair. That would take more investigation. Then there was the nurse and someone on the dining staff to consider as well.

"Look, Mrs. Billings, Pete was a good guy, but he did have an eye for women, and he may have broken a few hearts, but, like I said, I quit paying attention to his affairs." He stood and offered his hand. "I'm more than happy to help, and I'm glad you're nosing around, but I have to get back to work. This is the time I usually take Mrs. Sims to the activity room. She likes to play Canasta with a few other ladies."

I jumped up and shook his hand. "Oh, I'm sorry. I don't mean to keep you from your duties, but thank you so much for the information you shared."

He left, but I remained for a few minutes and mulled over what he'd told me. I had some new information, but it only served to clear up some questions and not really lead me to a killer. The one unknown factor still remained—the mystery woman with the rock.

Now I needed some new names, so I could compare them with the notes I had on the other woman. Of course, there was always the possibility that Lenny had made up that part, and he was the real killer. Then there was the business of the earring again. That could either lead me to the killer or it could simply be a case of an earring lost by someone out walking, especially since I had no idea how long it had been wherever Mitzi found it.

When I left the library and crossed the foyer, the first thing I noticed was that Carrie wasn't at the reception desk. The substitute was there instead.

"Hello, Mrs. Benson. I wasn't expecting to see you here today."

"Carrie had a few days off coming, so she took them, and I'm filling in for her. She'll be back next Monday."

"Well, I'm glad you're here. Have a good day."

I turned and headed back outside and home. My brain was on overload, and I needed chocolate to clear it up. Maybe Harry and Ben could help download it all if we put our heads together this afternoon.

On my walk back to my cottage, that illusive little bit of information kept darting in and out of my memory, but I couldn't get a grip on it to make it stay. Maybe that dark chocolate bar stashed in the pantry would clear the cobwebs.

Chapter 16

After I took care of Mitzi's needs, I grabbed a chocolate bar, my pad, and a pencil. If I didn't write down everything from this morning, I might not remember later on. Steve's information had helped clear up a few things, but not the mystery of the third woman who argued with Pete.

I wrote down what I knew about each woman. Maria had argued with Pete in the employees' locker room before he went out to work. Her keys were found later in the flower bed, but she said she left them in her purse in her locker. When she went to get them later, they were gone. I believed her story. Besides, her duties kept her too busy to be outside arguing with Pete again.

Then Taryn had gone out to see him, and they had argued about the flowers for the Harvest Dinner. She has long, dark hair, but she was the one wearing the red sweater and black pants that day. Besides, Lenny said she went back inside before the other woman came out. Still, I didn't want to rule her out. Lenny said the second woman had on dark clothes, and Taryn had worn black pants. She could have come back outside wearing a black jacket over her sweater.

I put her back on my list and concentrated again on what else I knew. Our day nurse has brown hair she wears in a twist at the back or a braid when she's at work, but I have seen it loose on her shoulders. She could have gone out in street clothes and then changed into her uniform later. I didn't remember her ever doing that before, but it remained a possibility.

I couldn't rule out Noreen either. She fit the description, and she could easily have had another pair of earrings like the ones I saw her wearing and lost one of them.

Carrie had dark hair and liked to wear it in a braid as well. What was she wearing that day? I couldn't remember, but then I hadn't been looking for the color of anyone's clothing that day.

By the time lunch rolled around, I had made some progress, but didn't have concrete evidence. I prepared a lunch of soup and a grilled cheese sandwich and sat down to enjoy it. Before I had taken two bites, Bessie yelled through the door and pounded on it.

I let her in, and she patted her chest with her hand to catch her breath. "The police are up at the main building. We have to get up there and see what's going on. It must be about Pete's murder, and they're here to arrest someone."

"Slow down, Bessie. They're probably here to ask more questions. "

"I don't know, but I saw Ben and Harry going in the door, so I came to get you."

If Ben and Harry were checking things out, I

wanted to be there, too. "Okay, let me get my jacket and I'll come with you."

A few minutes later we entered the lobby, and Detective Forester was there talking to Noreen. Ben and Harry were seated not far away, so we joined them. The first thing I noticed was that Ben wasn't wearing his sling. Either his shoulder was much better or he didn't want to wear it and I voted for the latter.

"What's going on Ben?" I sat beside him on the couch in the reception area. I leaned toward him. "Where's your sling?"

"It got in my way, and I didn't really need it anymore."

Just like a man to think like that. I glared at him, but he paid it no mind.

"I'm not sure why we're here. Harry and I found out that Steve has been out of town and didn't return until this week-end."

"I talked with him today and realized he couldn't have done it, so that leaves us with the women." I kept glancing toward Noreen and Forester who were in a serious discussion.

Noreen nodded in my direction, and the detective turned to lock gazes with me. He said something to Noreen before heading toward me.

"Mrs. Billings, I have a few more questions for you and your friends here."

Bessie's eyes opened wide, and she fanned her face with her fingers. "I don't know anything." She jumped up, well not quite, but she stood as fast as she could.

"I need to go check on my friend." She scurried

away like a mouse after seeing a cat.

The detective shook his head. "I didn't have her on my list anyway, but I do need to talk to the three of you."

Ben, Harry, and I glanced at one another. What had happened now?

"Harry, we checked out that car you said was parked behind Mrs. Billings' house, and we located the driver. One problem—he's disappeared." Then he looked straight at me.

"A neighbor said she saw him talking with a woman at the curb near his car yesterday afternoon. That woman fits your description. Were you at Lenny's place yesterday?"

Heat rushed up neck. Caught red-handed. "Um, yes I did find him and talk with him."

The detective shook his head. "Mrs. Billings, why in the world were you looking for him in the first place?"

"I found out that it was his car parked next to mine that morning. I just wanted to know whose it was. I gave the license plate number to Harry to find out for me."

The detective gave Harry a scathing look then and pointed his finger at him. "You had a license plate number and didn't give it to us?"

"Yes, I did, but I was only helping out a friend. I turned it in as soon as I realized it could be connected to Pete's murder."

The detective shook his head and glared at the three of us. "I appreciate your interest, but please quit interfering with our investigation. Now we have to spend more time looking for the man and finding out why he was here."

"Oh, I can tell you that." Maybe my information would put me in a better position.

He blew out his breath and took out a pad. "Okay, tell me what you know."

I proceeded to tell him everything about my visit with Lenny, including the women he claims he saw.

"That's all very interesting and useful, but there are a lot more questions we have for him, and he's disappeared from his home, his work, and anywhere else he might hide out. We know the right questions to ask and could perhaps have learned more about Lenny's business dealings with Pete."

"I'm sorry." And I was, but it didn't mean I'd quit my sleuthing. However, he was right. He could have gleaned a lot more answers with the right questions.

"It'd be best if you'd leave the solving of this crime to us, Mrs. Billings."

"I understand." The stern look didn't deter me one bit from what I still needed to do.

When he turned his attention to Harry, I saw that as my opportunity to get away and go back to my pad and pen. Besides, my stomach reminded me I hadn't finished my lunch.

I leaned toward Ben. "I'm going back to my place to eat my lunch. Let me know if anything of significance is said."

He gave me one of those looks that told me he knew what I was up to, but he didn't say anything, so I skedaddled out of there. After I freed Mitzi, I grabbed my pad and pen and went to work. I had my suspicions about the mystery woman, but I'd have to wait until all the regular staff was back on duty to ask any more questions.

Then I remembered all that was going on in the next few days. When would I ever find the time to do some more nosing around? Between the bridge tournament and the fall dinner, I had my hands full. Harry and I still hadn't had any time for practice games. Just the thought of it wore me out.

I finished lunch and spent the rest of the afternoon taking care of chores like changing my linens and doing the laundry. I also did a little baking. Those are the tasks that leave my mind free to explore and find answers to questions or problems I'm trying to solve.

After taking the last batch of cookies from the oven, I still hadn't come any closer to solving the mystery of the last woman to argue with Pete.

While they cooled, I turned my attention to the dinner coming up on Saturday. I had all the supplies I needed and the manpower to take care of them. Notices had been posted, and the candidates for the Harvest King and Queen would be announced later this evening. The kitchen and wait staff would take care of the clean-up of the dishes, but my committee would take care of taking down all decorations. At least we could leave the flowers on the table for Sunday and into next week.

Harry and I had neglected our game to the point we may not win over Ben and Bessie, and I didn't like that idea. I simply didn't want to listen to his bragging until the next tournament, so that had to planned for as well.

A knock on the door followed by Ben calling out my name let me know he and Harry had arrived. I opened the door and let them in.

Harry started in on me right away. "Boy, that Detective Forester wasn't very happy with you."

"What about you? You could have at least warned me." I held my anger at bay but crossed my arms over my body and glared at him.

"Sorry about that, but after you told us about your visit, I figured Lenny would lay low. If that was the case, the police would have a much better chance at finding him than I would."

There was some logic to that, but I still wasn't too pleased.

"Look, I know he told you to stop meddling, but that's not going to keep you from nosing around anyway. I'm sorry I didn't warn you, but I still want to help you and Ben with this."

He was right that I wouldn't stop asking questions, we could use his help. I sure wasn't getting that far on my own. "Okay, but we have to let each other know what we're doing." I fingered the earring in my pocket. I hadn't exactly been honest myself.

I pulled it out and opened my hand to show it. "I know I should probably have given this to Noreen to post in Lost and Found, or maybe I should even give it to the police, but I want to do some snooping and see what I can find. I know it came from a guy at a craft booth at War Eagle. Noreen said he doesn't sell them any place else. Something is floating around in my brain about it, but I can't quite reel it in yet."

Ben poured himself a cup of coffee and sat back on a stool. "That leads me to believe it does belong to one of the staff. Most of our residents don't have access to their own cars to go off on a shopping trip."

I held back a snicker. "Good deduction, Mr. Hot Shot Lawyer. I figured that out as soon as I knew it came from a craftsman at a show."

Harry held up his hand. "Now wait a minute. That's all a good theory, but it could easily have been a gift to one of our residents from a friend or family member."

I hadn't really considered that aspect, but it could be. That was why I couldn't stop trying to find out about anyone else Pete had been dating, and who owned the earring.

"You're right. It probably doesn't mean a thing." I slipped the earring into the drawer at the end of the table. I was still going to find out who lost it.

Chapter 17

That night during dinner, Taryn picked up a portable mike and called out for our attention. It was time to find out who had been nominated for Harvest King and Queen. We'd had ballots available for the past week to write down two names and turn them in. Electric excitement of anticipation charged the air, and even I wanted to know whose names were on the list.

Taryn read the list as murmurs of approval and applause resounded. She called out the last two names, and I nearly fell out of my chair. Ben and I had made the list. Bessie squealed, and Doris beamed her approval.

Laughter spilled from me before I could stop it. "I don't believe it. How did we get on there?"

Ben huffed out a breath and sat up taller. "Speak for yourself, my friend. I'm not surprised in the least. Why shouldn't we be on it?"

Bessie waved her hand in the air. "Abigail! Think about it. You do more around here than anyone else, and everyone knows you. The one I really can't understand being on there is Tillie, but I'm glad that nice Oren Hudson is."

"I must say it's an impressive list, and I'm

honored to be on it." I grabbed the cup of coffee I'd just sugared and sipped it. I peered over at Ben and hoped this new development wouldn't slow us down from hunting for more clues about our mystery woman.

Ben shook his head to let me know he understood my silent communication. Strange, the more we were together, the more we thought alike. A shiver scooted down my spine. I couldn't afford to get that close to any man, especially Ben Martin.

Bessie clapped her hands. "I know, let's all go out to lunch tomorrow and celebrate Ben and Abigail's nominations.

I groaned because I would have to go this time. I'd backed out with something else to do the last few times something like this luncheon idea came up.

Clara spoke her mind as usual. "Well, I suppose we should be honored to have two of the candidates for Harvest King and Queen sitting at our table. If you ask me, it's just a time-wasting frivolity."

Bessie raised her eyebrows. "Clara Bivens, you said yourself last week how much fun we'd have. You were even excited about Abigail's asking us to help with the decorations and stuff."

"Humph. That was then, this is now."

My heart went out to Clara. She'd actually been talked about as being a nominee, so this must have been a big disappointment to her. How could I soothe her ruffled feathers? "Clara, I don't know anyone who can arrange a table like you do. Taryn will be proud to have your talent put to use."

Clara sniffed. "Well, as long as we're doing it, we may as well do it right."

Doris Barton blinked her eyes against the moisture now filling them. "Pete's murder hasn't been solved yet, and we're still having a party. Sometimes I think this place just isn't serious enough in seeing that the murderer is caught."

Ben attempted to soothe Doris' feelings. "I understand how upset you are about all this, but Abby, Harry, and I are doing everything possible to see Pete's murder solved."

Doris said nothing, only pressed her lips together.

I had hoped the dinner would take everyone's mind off the murder, and I prayed now that more people didn't feel like Doris.

Clara returned to the idea of the lunch together. "Since we're going to do this, I know just the place for celebration. You men will like it too. They serve big portions that will fill a man's stomach for sure."

Bessie giggled. "I know where you mean. I can never eat it all, so I always bring a little box of food home with me. For the next day, you know." She leaned toward Ben, her words thick as maple syrup. "You and Harry will love the food at the Gazebo. Their sandwiches are big and hearty, and the desserts would tempt any man as big and strong as you are."

Ben almost dropped his fork. "Gazebo? That sounds like one of those tearooms with dainty china and tiny teacups. I don't care for those places."

Clara patted his hand. "Now, Ben, don't jump to conclusions. This isn't a ladies' type of place.

Why they even have chicken fried steak, fried catfish and all the trimmings."

"I hope so, and the desserts better be as good as you say. Those tearooms make me feel like a giant in a dollhouse."

The three ladies laughed and shook their heads. Doris shoved her napkin onto the table. "Now that's a good one, Ben, I'll have to remember it. But I've been there, and I think you'll be pleasantly surprised."

Harry spoke up. "I have some things to do in the morning, but I'd be happy to take everyone. I'll start picking everyone up at noon and go to Abby's last like we did for Peter's funeral."

"Sounds fine to me, and we can talk more about it at breakfast." Maybe by then I'd come up with an excuse not to go.

The other ladies nodded in agreement as well, and Clara stood. "Now that's settled, I'll see all of you at breakfast. Right now, I'm going to join some friends in a few games of Canasta."

After that, we all went our separate ways, except Ben followed me outside. "I guess the lunch idea isn't so bad. I went once or twice to one of those tearoom places with Millie just to make her happy."

"I understand. Jack did the same for me. With the voting the next two days, we won't have much time to worry about who is elected, but it also means we'll have other responsibilities for the dinner, so that cuts out our sleuthing time."

"Yes, but we can still ask questions and make observations." Suddenly I went down, and pain shot through my foot and ankle.

Ben grabbed me. "What's the matter? Are you okay?"

Harry ran up to us. "What happened? I saw Abby stumble."

"I hit the edge of the sidewalk and turned my ankle. It hurts like the dickens."

Ben and Harry lowered me to the grass. Ben picked up my foot. Even in the dim light of dusk the swelling was obvious. He loosened the ties on my shoe and eased it off. I winced and sucked in my breath.

"I think you have a bad sprain. We need to get you to the clinic and get this looked at."

"Oh, no, let's go back to my place, and I'll ice it down. I'll be okay." I didn't have time to waste on the clinic. Even if we did have a medical staff member on duty twenty-four hours, going to the clinic still took time.

Ben wore that determined look of his, but I wasn't going to give in. "I'm not going anywhere but home, and if you think otherwise, I'll go by myself."

"Okay. Be stubborn if you like, but don't blame us if it's more serious than a sprain."

Ben nodded to Harry and they helped me to my feet. Ben held my arm on the left side. "Do you have an Ace bandage you can wrap around it?"

"I think so. Just get me back, and I'll take care of it." For once I didn't mind leaning on him for support.

They were able to get me back to my house. Once inside, they eased me onto the recliner and made sure my foot was elevated. Ben hurried into the kitchen and found a large zip-lock bag and filled it with ice. Then he wrapped it in a towel and knelt beside me to wrap the bag around my ankle.

Mitzi barked, and I remembered I'd left her in her crate. Harry came back into the room with a bottle of aspirin and a small paper cup of water. "Here, I found these in the bathroom. They should help with the pain. Mitzi sure wasn't happy to see me. Should I let her out?"

"No, I'll take care of her later."

"Oh, and I looked, but didn't find a bandage."

I was sure I had one around somewhere, but if it wasn't in my bathroom cabinet, I didn't. I swallowed the aspirin and a sip of water.

Ben took the cup from me. "She's going to need one for sure. She's in no shape to go get one, but I can. I'll go to the drug store and get a bandage, or you can go, and I'll stay here."

Harry hesitated a moment before grinning. "I'll go. Mind if I take your car, Abby? It'll save time from having to walk down to my place and get mine."

"Sure. The keys are on the hook by the back door. You might get something a little stronger than aspirin while you're at it."

"Will do. See you two in a bit." He snagged the keys from the hook and headed out the door.

After he left, Ben went to the kitchen. "I'm going to make some coffee. That always seems to help things."

"No, Ben. I'd prefer a cup of chamomile tea instead. The tea bags are in the pantry, and you can heat the water in the microwave."

"Hot tea it is."

He reached for the pantry door, and I realized all my junk food lay in plain sight on the shelves. Before I could protest, he had it open.

Five seconds hadn't passed when I heard his raucous laugh. He poked his head around the pantry door. "For a health food nut, you sure have a lot of the good stuff lying around. I'll have to remember that next time I want a snack."

"Ben Martin, if you tell a soul about that, I'll never speak to you again."

He appeared holding the box of tea bags. "Your secret is safe with me, but just remember, I do know."

I leaned back in the recliner. This was not the way I had planned to spend my evening. We still had so much to do for the dinner Saturday night, and we were getting so close to finding out who killed Pete. I sure couldn't do much sleuthing with this ankle hurting like it was. I moved slightly to get more comfortable and had to grit my teeth against the pain shooting up my leg.

I took a deep breath and tried to get comfortable. Ben brought the tea, and after a few sips, I began to relax and my muscles went limp. A few minutes rest and I'd feel much better.

By the time Harry returned, the aspirin had lessened the pain, but I still welcomed his expert wrapping of my ankle.

"Thank you. I think it'll be much better now."

"Hmm, I got something else for you too." He reached behind him and produced a pair of crutches." I went over to my place and picked these up. They're left from when I had my broken leg last year. Glad I kept them now. I adjusted them a few inches to fit your height."

He and Ben helped me to stand on my good foot. "At least you'll be able to get around your house by yourself."

"Thank you. These will come in handy." I positioned them under my arms and took a few tentative steps. It had been long time since I'd been on crutches. "I think I'll remember how to do this without any trouble. I just have to remember to use my hands and not my arm pits."

Ben chuckled. "You got it." He reached over and picked up his jacket. "Harry, old friend, I think it's time for us to leave the lady to get some rest. After all, we have a big day ahead of us tomorrow."

Abby shuddered. "The luncheon. I forgot." Now I had a good excuse to stay home. "Maybe I shouldn't go tomorrow. You know, stay here and rest."

Harry laughed, and Ben shook his head. "Oh no, if I'm going, you are. It's in our honor, so you have to go."

I waved one of the crutches. "Thanks a lot."

Ben ducked and dashed for the door with Harry right behind him. He glanced back at me. "Don't forget to lock your door."

"Thank you, Harry, I will." Now all I had to do was get over there. After turning the dead bolt, I thumped my way to the bedroom. Mitzi yipped like crazy.

I opened her crate and she leapt out at me and

almost caused me to fall. "Whoa, sorry there, sweetie, but we have to be more careful."

She sat back on her haunches and eyed me with her head turned to one side. Hopping about on one foot, I managed to get my pajamas out and changed into them.

After taking care of my nightly routine and letting Mitzi out, I waited by the back door for her to do her business. Some evening this had turned out to be, but it had been rather nice to have two people caring about me. No one had really been around to look after me since Jack's death.

I buried the thought and closed the door when Mitzi returned. I crawled into bed and pulled up the covers. No matter how nice it had been tonight, I didn't want it to become a habit. I valued my independence too much.

Chapter 18

The next morning, I skipped breakfast. I didn't feel like trying to walk up to the main building with my crutches. I rested all morning, and promptly at noon, Harry arrived with his SUV. Doris and Clara had managed to get to the back seat so I could be in the middle one with Bessie. Clara gave the directions to Harry, and we took off. The other women chattered on about the menu at The Gazebo, but my thoughts kept going over what we did and didn't know in Pete's murder.

I had planned to interview a few other staff members, especially the nurse and Carrie, this morning, but now that would have to wait. Mrs. Benson had said Carrie took a few days off, and my curiosity bade me to find out why. She had never taken time off except for vacations.

The tearoom was exactly as it had been described. Even Ben was impressed. The hostess smiled and led us to a round table in a corner overlooking a beautiful garden.

Ben and Harry assisted us ladies with our chairs and Ben sat next to me. "This place is very nice. It looks like a tearoom, but it has something about it that keeps it from being what my teen-age granddaughter calls 'girlie, girlie.' If you know what I mean."

"Yes, I do." Ben was right about the décor. Beautiful antiques provided a variety of table types and chairs as well as paintings and mirrors on the walls. The predominant color of blue made up tablecloths and napkins and a number of the chairs were upholstered in the color. Contrasted with the white woodwork, the color scheme gave a very pleasant environment for dining.

The menu delighted me even more. My favorite quiches and sandwiches as well as salads appealed to me, but heartier soups and even a few grilled meats rounded out the items offered to entice heartier appetites.

Harry grinned and held his menu straight up between his hands. "Now this is more like it. I don't see fat-free, sugar-free, or caffeine-free anywhere."

The young lady now placing crystal goblets of water at our places said, "Oh, we have those on a special list. I can get you one if you'd like."

"Not on your life. What we have here is perfect."

After everyone ordered, the talk turned to the dinner tomorrow night and the decorations. Since I had bought so many smaller items, I was grateful I would have help getting the tables all done. We had thirty-six tables in our dining hall, and I had assigned ten each to Bessie, Clara, and Doris. No one else had responded to the call we put on the bulletin board for volunteers, so we'd get it done alone.

"Abigail, what do you think?"

I blinked my eyes and peered at Clara. "I'm sorry. What do I think about what?"

"See, I told you she wasn't paying attention. We were talking about Pete and were wondering about the rumors we'd heard. Do you think he really was dating so many different women at Spring Hills? If he was, it looks like he might have had a number of people wanting him dead. Jealous girlfriends and all that."

I almost choked on the tea I sipped. Where in the world did they come up that information? I had come to the same conclusion earlier, but I didn't want to share my thoughts on that just yet. "I suppose that could be the case, but we also know he was a gambler and bragged about winning big. I believe several of our residents had given Pete money to bet at the tables for them, and if he lost a lot, they'd have reason to kill him as well."

The three ladies jumped on that like a kitten after a ball of yarn. I cut my eyes to Ben at my side with what I hoped he saw as a need to change the subject.

He got the message and nodded. "Ladies, let's talk about the bridge tournament coming up. Bessie and I are going to win it all again this year."

Of course, Harry had to protest and that led to argument between him and Ben. I listened to them bicker and tease as our meals were served. Jealousy could very well have been the motive for Pete's murder and would explain what he and that third woman argued about.

When we finished eating, we headed back to the car and sat in the same arrangement as before.

Once we settled, I leaned forward to whisper to Ben. "We need to meet. Can you come in about an hour?"

Ben nodded. "I'll tell Harry. You have a new idea?"

"Not yet, but several keep skirting around in my head, and I want to discuss them with you."

I settled back in my seat, and Bessie shot me a look I couldn't quite describe. She didn't hesitate to speak her mind. "You and Ben planning a special date after we get back? You two have been spending a lot of time together."

How was I to answer that? If I told her we were working on Pete's murder, she'd want all the details, and then the rest of the complex would know what we were doing. That could lead to getting me into more trouble with the police. "No, I'm trying to get him to meet me for golf." Maybe a little white lie wouldn't hurt too much. I almost punched Ben when he had a coughing spasm to hide his laughter. Bessie raised her eyebrows, and her expression certainly questioned my statement.

I didn't think any more about it until after we arrived back at Spring Hills. Ben stayed with me on the pretext that he wanted to help me navigate my crutches. When the SUV pulled away, he shook his head. "Those women will talk your arms and ears off. I'm glad we're only together a short time at breakfast and dinner each day. And what was that bit about golf? That was about as far-fetched as it comes, especially with you on crutches."

Heat rushed up my neck. "I didn't even think of that, but I had to say something to get Bessie's mind off us, and that was the first thing to come to mind."

No wonder she'd looked at me with raised eyebrows. That's what I get for letting my mouth speak before I think about the words. I led him inside, and he offered to take Mitzi outside for me. That was both a surprise and a relief. I hadn't relished the idea of taking care of my dog on crutches, but Ben usually avoided anything to do with Mitzi. When he brought her back inside, Harry followed him.

After I settled Mitzi with a few doggie treats, I got down to business. "Okay, partners, let's get our notes and ideas on the table and see what we come up with." I reached for my handy pad and pen. Ben grinned, and Harry shook his head. Neither of them can understand why I don't use my phone or tablet to take notes and keep records. I suppose I'm old-fashioned and want the feel of the pen as I write. Helps me remember better, too.

Harry leaned back in his chair. "I don't know why we're doing this. We don't know any more today than we did yesterday or the day before."

"We need to review what we have. We're missing something somewhere." I tried to focus on the one fact that kept darting in and out but with nothing I could pinpoint. I reached into the drawer in the table and pulled out the earring.

"There's something I keep missing, and I think it has to do this even though Mitzi didn't find it until a day or so later, and I have no idea where she found it or how long it'd been there."

Harry held out his hand. "May I look at it?"

I handed it to him, and he turned it over in his

hand. "It can't have been there very long because the silver isn't tarnished. It just has a little dirt around the edges of the setting."

He gave it back to me. "I notice it's one of those that clip on instead of the hook for pierced ears. Makes it easier to lose."

"Yeah, I know. I've lost more than my share. I don't know why anyone would want to punch holes in their bodies to stick things in. Noreen Jenson's are like this, but she still has hers and wore them the other day." I tapped the earring with my finger. "This has to be the clue."

Ben stood and stretched. "Well, keep thinking on it. I'm going home for a nap. Maybe I'll be able to think better after a little snooze."

Harry joined him, and he clasped my shoulder. "You're a smart woman, Abby, and whatever it is you need to find, you will."

With that they both left with me still sitting with the earring in my hand. If only Mitzi could tell me exactly where she'd found it. I sighed. Well, that wasn't going to happen. I pushed back from the table, reached for my crutches and hobbled to the pantry for my stash of junk snacks. They'd certainly help my mood even if they didn't help me remember.

Chapter 19

On Saturday morning, a throbbing pain awakened me. I'd spent too much time on my feet yesterday and paid for it this morning. The pills taken before bed last night had worn off. I reached for the bottle on my nightstand, poured out two, and swigged them down with a gulp of water. I glanced at the clock and moaned. It was already six-thirty. Time to get up and start my daily routine, but my down pillow beckoned me to snuggle back under the covers and sleep.

Christian music poured from the clock radio and reminded me that I needed to spend time with the Lord. I pushed the covers aside and sat on the side of the bed. After sliding my good foot into one slipper, I decided to forget the other one. It was still too swollen. Instead, I pulled on the slipper sock worn the night before. I grabbed the crutches leaning against the night table and positioned them under my arms.

Mitzi yipped about my ankles. "I know I'm slow, but I'll get your breakfast and let you out soon as I can." I clunked my way into the kitchen where the aroma of coffee aroused me from my groggy state.

Thankful for the automatic timer on the coffee maker, I poured a cup of the hot brew and savored the sweet caffeine aroma. After taking a sip, I hobbled to the pantry and filled Mitzi's food bowl and checked the other one for water. With that accomplished, I sank onto a chair at the table and pulled my Bible toward me.

The Bible passage for the morning devotional thought centered on ever-present love of God. As I read the eighth chapter of Romans, I marveled anew at the power of the Lord. As much as I hated spraining my ankle, everything works for good for those who love the Lord, and I did love the Lord, so something good must be ahead.

The Harvest dinner was tonight, and I needed to be in good spirits while we decorated and prepared for all the fun Taryn had planned. *Lord, please don't let me put a damper on everything tonight.*

I wouldn't make a pretty picture with my crutches and bandaged up ankle, but there was nothing I could about that now. I returned to my Bible. The more I read, the more the pain lessened. Now I could face whatever the day decided to throw at me. It certainly hadn't given me anything new in the past two days.

My thoughts kept returning to that earring. It had to be the final clue. If not, we'd all be back at practically square one. I had several more people to interview and after Ben's suggestion about other staff members Pete dated. I also needed to find time to question Taryn further.

I hadn't been to the main building since my

little mishap. After the big lunch yesterday, handling those crutches simply wasn't worth all the effort to go over for dinner. But today was special, and I wanted to be there to supervise all the plans we'd put together. After lunch, the dining hall would be transformed into a wonderland of fall colors and decorations. As much as I wanted to help, I had to settle for the reality that I couldn't do much but offer suggestions.

Somehow today, while at the main building, I needed to snoop a little more. Maybe one of the tenants had actually lost the earring. A knock on the door brought me out of her thoughts. I wasn't expecting visitors this time of morning. I thumped into the living room and opened the door.

Ben grinned back at me. "I thought you might need a little help this morning, so I went up and borrowed a wheel chair from the clinic. Save you having to manage those crutches all the way up to breakfast."

He never ceased to amaze me with his thoughtfulness. All the teasing had been in fun, but his kind gestures were more serious business. Chagrin for the way I had treated him on various occasions rippled through my soul. How could I have been so blind to his sincere caring?

"Thank you. That's so thoughtful." My independence was still important to me, but relying on the help of others at the moment wasn't such a bad thing after all.

"I just wanted to be sure you didn't injure that ankle again. It's what any friend would do. You about ready to go?"

"Yes, I am." I eased into the chair and positioned the crutches at my side. Helping out a friend? Did he really think of me only as a good friend? Maybe I misinterpreted his actions of the past.

Ben grasped the handles and pushed. "Well, looks like we won't meet our goal of solving the murder this week, but the police haven't made any progress either from what Harry says."

"I know, and I'm rather disappointed we haven't. I still have a few people I want to question. Carrie and the day nurse are two of Pete's past relationships, and I bet there are more."

"That wouldn't surprise me since he was so attracted to the ladies."

I snickered, and Ben growled. I twisted around to see his grimace.

When we entered the main building, the sight of me in the wheelchair drew others to my side wanting to know what happened and how I was feeling.

After the fifth explanation, I grabbed Ben's hand. "Please make some kind of announcement or something. I don't want to tell this story over and over again.

He laughed. "Okay, that's a good idea."

After I was seated at our table, Ben laid my crutches by my side and wheeled the chair out of the way. He made his way around a few of the tables and told them the same thing I'd been saying. A few looked my way, so I smiled and waved back at them.

He returned to the table to tell me what he'd

said. "I told them you'd sprained your ankle when we were walking home the other night, and that you appreciated their concern, but you're much better now." He glanced around the room. "Now, let's enjoy our breakfast."

"Thank you, Ben. Maybe that will cut down on the questions."

"Well, they still had one I couldn't answer." He reached for the bowl of scrambled eggs. "They all wanted to know when you're going to find out who killed Pete."

"I hope you told them you didn't know because I sure don't."

Bessie leaned over to speak. "I'll be glad when this all over, too. What if we do have a killer running loose around here? None of us would be safe."

Clara pursed her lips and narrowed her eyes. "We know you're still trying to solve Pete's murder even though the police said to stay out of it. I think you're making a mistake in nosing around. What if you make the killer angry and he comes after you?"

I hadn't really thought about that, but I doubted it would happen. "We don't know if the killer is a man or woman, but I'm not worried either way."

Bess gave me one of those looks that let me know she'd have a word or two to say later before she said, "The rest of us will take care of everything this afternoon. You'll need to stay off your feet as much as possible, or you won't be able to enjoy the party tonight."

I couldn't argue with that, but I did want to be there to help them organize everything. "I'll do that, but not without helping out a little while."

"All right, if you insist." She shook her finger at me. "But I'm telling you, we're sending you home early."

After that the talk returned to other topics about the dinner that night. They all had their speculations about who would win. Our group supported Ben and me, but deep down, I hoped someone else would win. Ben and I didn't need the extra attention. We needed to keep focused on solving Pete's murder.

Later that afternoon, I thumped my way over to the main building on my crutches. Ben would probably fuss at me, but I didn't care. He could save the wheelchair for me to use tonight.

The flowers had been delivered, and they were beautiful. The florist had followed the order to perfection. The gold, yellow, and bronze mums had been arranged in brass containers and filled in with brown magnolia leaves. The tables would look as festive as I imagined.

Bessie, Doris, and Clara bustled in and made a beeline for the large cart containing all the decorations I'd purchased at the craft store.

The wait staff had exchanged the usual white cloths for burnt orange ones to go with the decorations. They now placed the china and flatware on each table. The florist made her way around the tables to place the flowers in the center of each one.

I felt as useless as a wet noodle sitting around watching everyone else decorate the dining area. Bessie and Doris bustled about helping the staff to place napkins and silverware on the tables. Even Clara worked in getting everything set up for tonight. The mum centerpieces in their brilliant hues sat on each table with scarecrows and candles to complete the array. It all came together just like I had imagined.

Being on crutches put a damper on everything I wanted to accomplish this day, but they seemed to be doing just fine without me.

Across the way I spotted Noreen Jensen in conversation with one of the staff members. Noreen shook her head as though frustrated about something. A few minutes later she disappeared into her office. Now what was that all about? Maybe it was because Carrie hadn't come back to work yet. I sure wanted to speak with that young lady myself.

Since they only had a few tables left to decorate, I decided to find out why Carrie had not returned. I stood and balanced on my crutches.

Bessie hurried over to me. "Oh, Abby, I do hope your ankle won't too much trouble for you tonight."

"Thank you, dear. I'm sure I'll be fine. Right now, I feel like the odd man out, so I'm going back to my place and rest for this evening."

Bessie's curls bounced. "That's a good idea. We'll take care of things here." She hustled away with her armload of table decorations.

Before I could leave for my mission, Taryn hurried into the room and waved an envelope in the air. I sat back down and waited for her to come to me.

When she got to me, she thrust the envelope

into my hands. "Here are the pictures from last year. I thought you'd like to see them and maybe get a few ideas."

I didn't know what difference they could make now that we were well on our way with the decorating, but I took them. May as well see what they looked like.

"Thank you, Taryn. Let's look at them over on that empty table." I managed to hold on to the envelope and make it to the table. There we spread the pictures out and examined them.

Most of them were of tables filled with our people, all smiling and happy for the camera. I noticed a few close-ups and picked up a few. I couldn't stop my grin at the one of Ben and me at our table. We did make a fine-looking couple. I shoved it aside to keep from going down that rabbit trail and picked up the next one.

My mouth dropped open, and a gasp escaped before I could capture it and hold it back.

"Are you okay, Abigail?"

I blinked my eyes and cleared my throat. "I'm fine." I grasped the picture. "Do you mind if I borrow a few of these? I want to look at more, but I'm tired and need to go back to my cottage. I'll bring them back this evening."

"No that's fine." She quirked an eyebrow at me, but I had nothing more to say.

I gathered a few of the pictures in a way that wouldn't give her a clue as to the one I was really interested in examining further.

I spotted Ben finally arriving and motioned for him to come to me. When he reached me, I handed him the pictures. "Take these and walk back with me to my place. I need to check something."

Ben furrowed his brow and took the pictures from me. He waved at Harry. "I'm walking Abby back home. We'll see you when you finish."

I grinned and shook my head. "That ought to whet his curiosity."

Ben followed me out the door. "Okay, what's up? I can tell by the look in your eye that you're on to something.

"I think I may have just figured out who killed Pete."

Chapter 20

Ben stopped short and stared at me. "You did what?"

"I think I figured out who killed Pete. Now let's get to my cottage where we'll have some privacy. I'll tell you about it when we get there."

"It must have something to do with these pictures. I saw Taryn bring them in to you."

"Yes, but hush until we're inside." I picked up speed and made it to my door without him asking more questions.

Ben followed me. "Abby Billings, you're almost as fast on those crutches as you are walking. Slow down."

"Not until we're inside." I clomped up onto the porch and unlocked my door. Once inside, I made it over to the table and plopped down in a chair, worn out from the walk. "Ben, let Mitzi out. She should be okay, but she doesn't need to be cooped up in her box."

He shook his head, but went to her box and opened it. I heard him telling her to behave because I was too tired to take care of her. I had to chuckle at how he was talking to her now like I did. Ben had finally accepted Mitzi, and she responded to him now even better than she had before. Maybe the two of them would get along after all.

While I waited for Ben to return, I spread the pictures out, and then pulled the earring from the drawer. I held it in my closed fist when he came back to the table.

"Look at these pictures and see if you see the same thing I did."

He bent over and perused them for a few minutes before shaking his head and straightening up. "I just see our friends and some of the staff having a good time at last year's dinner."

I pointed to the one that had attracted my attention. "Look closely at this one."

"Hmm, I'm not sure, but . . ." He picked up the picture to examine it more closely. "She's wearing an earring that looks like the one you found."

"Yes! That's it!" I opened my fist. "Here, see, it's one and the same."

He studied them both again. "You're right. We have to let the police know about this for sure now." He laid the picture with the rest. "I'm going back to get Harry and Noreen. They both need to know about this. They can help us decide what to do with the information."

Before I could respond, he was through the door and on his way back up to the dining hall. I started thinking about all the other signs of something being wrong since Pete's death. This new suspect had been on the list of women Pete had been involved with in the past, and her behavior had been a little odd on more than one occasion since then.

We did need to let the detective know, but it would spoil the excitement of tonight. On the other hand, if we didn't, our suspect may disappear. I was sure glad I didn't have to make that decision alone.

In five minutes Ben returned with Harry and Noreen in tow. Harry blew out his breath and shook his head. "Now tell us what this is all about. Ben wouldn't tell us anything except you knew who killed Pete."

"Is that true, Abby? Do you really know who killed him?"

"I can't say for sure, Noreen, but Ben and I both agree it's suspicious. I just need to know what to do with the information."

I showed them both the picture and the earring and explained how I came to have the earring.

"Oh my, no wonder you had so many questions about mine like that. I remember now seeing her wear them to work before." Noreen chewed on her bottom lip. "This isn't good at all, but it looks like you're right."

"Okay, so what are we going to do about it? I sure don't want to spoil the fun for everyone tonight, but we do need to tell Detective Forester about it don't you think?"

Harry snapped his fingers. "Yes, we do, and I'll take care of that. I'll go down to the station now and explain to him what we suspect and know and tell him about the dinner tonight. Most likely he'll wait or do some investigating on his own before making any arrests."

"If he does, then the dinner can go off without a hitch. The only thing I'm worried about is her getting away. With this being the weekend and all, if the police start questions again, she might up and disappear." I wasn't sure that would happen with this woman, but we had to think of every possibility.

"Oh dear, that may be why she's taken off the past few days. We need to let that detective know soon as possible. She's supposed to be back at work on Monday, but that doesn't mean she will." Noreen jumped up from her chair. "I've got to get back and make sure everything's running smoothly for tonight. I also have an idea as to how to get her here."

"I'm leaving as well to head straight for the station." Harry picked up the picture and the earring. "I'm taking these with me to show Forester. He can decide what to do with them from there."

Ben patted my arm. "If you're sure you'll be okay, I'm going on back to help the ladies finish up. Don't want them to think I'm shirking my duties."

They all left me at the table still garnering my thoughts into a clearer picture. I patted Mitzi's head. "What could have made a woman so angry that she had to kill Pete? The only thing I could think of was jealousy. She probably didn't intend to kill him, but that's what happened, and whether or not it would make a difference was up to the police to decide.

Mitzi tilted her head and stared at me as though she knew she'd had a part in solving this mystery.

The question now was when and where would Detective Forester make the arrest. I sure didn't want the dinner tonight to be overshadowed by it. I had to trust Harry to do and say whatever would bring the best results.

After a quick nap, I dressed for the dinner. No word had come from Harry or Ben as to what would be done about Pete's murder. All kinds of scenarios ran through my mind, and none of them were very good. Then I had to remember, our suspect may not even be at the dinner tonight. It wasn't a requirement for her, and she'd been off a few days, so whatever happened with any arrests or confrontations may be nowhere near Spring Hills.

Ben arrived promptly at seven, ready to wheel me to our destination. After I settled in the chair, I was ready for some answers. "Do you know what Harry and Forester decided for tonight?"

He pushed me to the porch and turned to lock the door. "No. All Harry said was that it was all taken care of, and I trust him with that. So, let's go enjoy dinner with our friends."

Noreen Jensen met us at the door. "I'm glad to see you two. I wanted you to know she'll be here tonight. I asked Steve to do me a favor and ask her as a date. He did, and she accepted. I don't think she knows we're suspicious."

I pressed my hand to my chest. "That's good, but won't her arrest ruin the party?"

"No, Harry and that detective worked it out with me. You'll see. It'll be fine."

At this point all I could do was trust her and the others. Ben wheeled me into the dining room and over to our table. After I sat in my chair beside Bessie, Ben stored the wheelchair out of the way and joined us.

Oh how I wanted to quiz Harry as to what had

happened at the police station, but with the others sitting there, I kept my mouth shut. A tiny miracle for me with all that was going on behind the scenes.

Conversation ranged from the Bridge tournament coming up soon to who would be our new Harvest King and Queen. With everything else going on, I prayed it wouldn't be Ben or me.

I noticed Carrie was there, and she sat with some of the other staff members at a table on the other side of the room. She didn't look very happy even though those around her seemed to be enjoying the festivities.

After the comedian presented his program filled with jokes to which we could all relate. Taryn took to the microphone. All conversation ceased, and we waited for the big announcement. Four men and four women had been nominated, but Taryn didn't waste time with runners-up. After thanking the committee for the work they'd done and the staff for their part, she finally held up an envelope.

"Here are the names of our Harvest King and Queen for this year." She grinned and waved it around for a moment before opening it and pulling out the sheet. "This year's Harvest King and Queen are Oren Hudson and Elizabeth Greene."

I clapped hard right along with the rest of them with my heart thanking the Lord I hadn't been named. Elizabeth was quiet, but well loved by everyone, and I was happy for her and for Oren.

Ben didn't look all that pleased, so I poked him with my elbow. "We don't have time for this right now, so it's a good thing we weren't elected."

"I suppose you're right." He glanced over at

Harry as people began preparing to leave and return to their apartments or cottages. "Time to get our show on the road."

Harry stood and leaned toward me. "Follow me to Noreen's office."

Ben nodded, retrieved the chair and wheeled me to the office. Curiosity as to how this was all going to go down set my heart to pounding and nerves tangling. When we entered Noreen's office, she asked us to take our places around the room.

In the next moment, the door opened, and Steve entered with Carrie. At the sight of us in the room, her face blanched, and she stepped backward against Steve.

Carrie clutched her hands so that her knuckles turned white, but she took a seat by Noreen's desk. This whole thing didn't seem right, but I didn't exactly know for sure about proper procedures. I decided to sit quietly by and see what happened.

Noreen laid the earring on the desk. "Do you recognize this piece of jewelry, Carrie?"

Carrie pressed her hands into her lap and swallowed. She shook her head. "No, I don't think I've ever seen it before."

My mouth dropped open. Who was she trying to kid? I had proof the earring was hers.

Chapter 21

Harry glanced at me and our gazes locked. She was lying, and we knew it. However, he kept his face as blank as a fresh sheet of paper. That must be why he was such a good cop. He let the detective do his job.

Noreen turned the picture over. "Then how did you happen to be wearing them at last years' fall dinner?"

Carrie crumpled in her seat with tears filling her eyes.

Before either Ben or I could warn her, words spilled from her mouth. "I didn't mean to do it. I didn't even know Pete was dead until y'all told me later."

Noreen rose and went around the desk to kneel before Carrie. "Tell me what happened." She handed Carrie a tissue.

Carrie sniffed back her tears, and I wanted to go and hug her myself. She wasn't a bad person, and I did feel sorry for her. I wanted to hear her story as much as anyone right now.

"Pete broke up with me last spring. I thought he was getting serious and might ask me to marry him, but he left me instead. I started to quit my job so I wouldn't have to see him, but decided I liked it here too much to do that. I was still mad at him, but since our jobs didn't really bring us into contact, I decided to stay."

Noreen patted her arm. "I can understand that, honey, but why did you argue with him that day?"

Her tissue was in shreds by now, but she continued to tear at it. "I overheard him talking and then arguing with Maria about money for her little girl. Pete had won all that money and now he wanted to give it to her. I was furious. Then when everyone was at breakfast, I went out to confront him and found him at the flowerbeds by your cottage, Mrs. Billings."

I nodded and waited for her to continue.

"We got into an argument about what he was doing with his money, and he said it was none of my business. I said I didn't want to see Maria hurt like he'd hurt me. He actually laughed at me and said he loved Maria and he'd never loved me. Then he turned around to work on your azaleas."

The tears flowed freely now, and she had to stop to catch her breath before she continued. "That made me absolutely furious, so I picked up a rock from the flower bed and hit him from behind. He fell forward but I ran away and left him there. I thought he was alive and just stunned."

Noreen hugged her. "I'm so sorry, Carrie, but we have to let Detective Forester know. I wish you had come forward at the time and explained this."

"I couldn't. I was so afraid no one would believe me that I kept my mouth shut."

She looked at me, blinking back tears. "I'm so

sorry, Mrs. Billings, but I was so upset with you because you wouldn't leave things alone. That's why I finally had to take a few days off. When I found out about that thing in his stomach, it made me sick. I panicked because I knew y'all would think I did it."

She was right. If we'd known right away she was that mystery woman, we'd have turned her in without hearing her story. Now I wasn't so sure about anything.

Noreen rose to open the door and Forester entered. He glared at me, but then he smiled. "Thank you for giving us the last piece of evidence we needed for an arrest. I should be angry because you withheld it so long, and I was at first, but then Harry convinced me you couldn't have known it meant anything since it could have come from anywhere."

Just as well he didn't know I'd suspected it to be a clue from the very beginning. Noreen hid her smile, and I remembered our conversation about that very earring only last week. She knew the truth, but she wouldn't say anything.

Detective Forester approached Carrie with handcuffs. "Carrie Watkins, you're under arrest for the murder of Pete Simpson."

Carrie cringed and bowed her head. Detective Forester read her rights and said he was taking her down to the station for questioning.

Ben jumped up beside me. "Don't say another word, Carrie. I'm going with you. You need a good lawyer."

I gasped, and my mouth dropped open. I

couldn't believe my ears, but Ben was right. She did need a good lawyer, and he'd been among the best. Maybe things would work out after all.

After they left, I confronted Noreen. "How did Forester get here so quick?"

"He was already in the building. He arrived during the dinner saying he was here to see Carrie. We convinced him to wait until after the dinner so as not to alarm everyone and ruin their evening. He agreed to wait until now. I think he said something about other evidence, but I don't know what that may be. I'm glad Ben will be there to help her."

I was too. His reputation for being one to make sure the truth came out would be put to the test if this one went to trial.

I wheeled myself back to the dining room and our table. Bessie, Clara and Doris were all over me as soon as I arrived.

Bessie grabbed me by the arm. "We saw that detective guy leaving with Carrie and Ben. What happened? What's going on?"

Clara and Doris pulled up chairs, their faces eager to hear the news themselves. I explained what had happened and why Ben was with Carrie.

"Oh, that poor girl, I feel so sorry for her. She's not a cold-blooded killer." Bessie crossed her arms over her ample bosom. "I'm glad Ben is going to look out for her. She'll need a good attorney, and he's exactly that."

Doris pursed her lips and shook her head. "Well, I knew that gal was hiding something, but I never dreamed it was something like this. I guess we all assumed a man killed Pete."

And they had assumed wrong. I learned early on that assumptions would almost always send me in the wrong direction. That's why I had kept my eyes and ears open for the mystery woman.

"We'll have to wait and see what happens now. In the meantime, let's get this finished and get some rest. I'm worn out." And I was, but not so much from cleaning up as I was from all that had happened today. What I needed most right now was some time with the Lord and a good night's sleep.

I headed home and prepared for bed. I prayed for things to work out in a good way for Carrie, swallowed a pain pill, and turned over to sleep.

After a half-way decent night, I decided not to go up to the main building for breakfast. I also decided to go to my home church for services. I simply didn't feel like fielding a bunch of questions from everyone around here.

I did want to see Ben and ask him about last night but didn't want to walk down to his cottage. He'd have to come to me.

After coffee and a blueberry muffin, I dressed for church. At least my ankle didn't hurt as much as it did yesterday. Before I left, I gave Ben a call. He should be awake and dressed by now.

He didn't answer which led me to believe he must have gone up for breakfast. Then someone knocked, and when I opened the door, Ben stood on my porch.

"Where were you at breakfast? I had to try and answer all those questions myself without giving them all the details."

I couldn't help but laugh. "That's exactly why I

didn't go up there, and I bet it was Bessie wanting the details."

"You have that right. Anyway, I need to tell you what happened. Carrie is charged with involuntary manslaughter or negligent homicide here in Arkansas. She told the detectives the exact same story she told us.

"What we didn't know is that the crime scene team found the bloody rock. Even Harry didn't know that, and the autopsy report showed the blow to the head didn't kill him, but the aerator did. So, he died as a result of her actions, but she didn't have the intention to kill him when she hit him."

"I wish she hadn't waited so long to confide in us. We could have helped her then. Even if she was afraid of the police, she should've trusted us."

"I'm going back this afternoon. If I can negotiate a deal, she most likely will spend only a year in prison with a hefty fine."

"Who'll pay the fine? Does she have any family who can help her? We need to do what we can. Will she be out on bail?"

"The best deal we can make is one that will have her go directly to jail, pay the fine and serve her time which I hope we can get down to one year, maybe two. She's already contacted her family, and they'll be here today. There won't need to be a trial since she's already confessed. If we can get her before a judge in the next few days, we can take care of everything and get it over with."

That was good to hear, but I hated the thought of Carrie being in jail. I realized she had to pay for what she had done although Pete's death hadn't been intentional.

"Sounds like you've been busy, and I'm glad you were there for her. It'd be terrible to have to go through that alone."

"She'll be okay with her parents here." He furrowed his brow. "Were you on your way out?"

"Yes, I'm on my way to church. Want to come with me?"

"No, I'm going on back to my place. I have to be back at the station around one. That's when Mr. and Mrs. Watkins should arrive, and I want to be there. Enjoy the service, and I'll see you later this evening."

With that he left. If it hadn't been going to the police station, Ben would have had some other excuse for not attending church. Somehow, I needed to help him see the importance of God in our lives. Neither of us was getting any younger, and I sure didn't want him to meet his maker unprepared.

I secured Mitzi in her kennel. "I'm just going to church, so I'll be back in a little while." She gave me one of her sad-eyed looks, but I ignored it. She'd be fine until I got home.

At church, I was able to sit alone near the back and listen to what the preacher had to say this morning. His message was all about becoming a new creature in Christ and changing old ways. God forgives us for all our sins when we seek Him, and He's working on us every day.

I had no doubt the Lord had His hands full watching over me and forgiving my wayward ways, but that made me think of Ben. He wasn't much of a one for going to church, and I'd never really asked why or discussed it with him.

With Pete's murder now out of the way and in the hands of the professionals, maybe now it was time for me to take my faith more seriously and be concerned about others and their walk with the Lord. I hadn't been the best role model of faith, but that was going to change. If I couldn't walk my talk, I had no business trying to get Ben interested in the ways of the Lord.

All the way home I thought about Carrie and offered a prayer of thanks for her parents being with here for her. I'd have to make a special effort to visit with her if she actually ended up spending time in prison. She'd need friends more than ever.

After I ate lunch, I rested until Ben returned from his trip to the police station. He came inside all smiles, so all must have gone well.

"Looks like you've had a good day. Would you like coffee while you tell me about it?"

"Coffee sounds good. A cold front is coming through, and the air is nippy out there." He removed his coat and sat at the table.

"The DA offered a fair deal, and we took it. Her fine will be taken care of by her parents, and she'll spend eighteen months in prison, less if she qualifies for good behavior parole, and I think she will. One other thing I learned, she's the one who put Maria's keys in the flower bed after they'd taken Pete's body away, and the police had all left the scene."

"Well, that does explains a lot, but I'm so relieved to hear she has a light sentence. I prayed for her this morning, and I prayed for you to be able to help her in every way possible."

"Did you now? I'm not sure what good prayer will do for an old reprobate like me. I'm set in my ways, so it's little late for me to make changes, but thanks."

It looked like I had my work cut out for me, and it might take some time. Peace cuddled my heart. It was never too late to bring another soul into the fold or to bring it back.

COMING SOON, BOOK TWO – TO CATCH A THIEF

Chapter 1

"Abigail, did you hear we had another theft last night? Ellie Davenport's pearl and diamond necklace and earrings are missing." Bessie Johnson sat back with a satisfied grin as she shared the news. Everyone at the table stopped eating and stared at her and then at me. Bessie loved spreading news, bad or good, but this was not her usual tidbit of information.

I laid down my fork. "When did this happen?"

"I don't really know. I just saw her going into Mrs. Jenson's office and she told me. It must have happened last night because she had them on when I saw her right after dinner."

Ben Martin, seated next to me, guffawed. "We'd better hop over and help her find them. Her eyesight is so poor they could be in front of her face."

I glared at him. "Ben, what an awful thing to say. Poor Ellie. I'll bet she's worried sick. Those pearls belonged to her mother."

Bessie's perfectly coiffed and curled gray head bobbed in agreement. "She's so upset, and so is Kate Hughes. She still hasn't found her cameo brooch."

Conversation buzzed among the other five at the table, but I shut them out. Two thefts may have been accidental or attributed to other causes, but with Kate's, Ellie's was the fourth such disappearance in the past month, and way too many. Oddly enough, all of the thefts had occurred in the main building with individual apartments for assisted living and memory-care residents. Nothing had been reported out in the cottages where I and the others at my table lived.

Harry should have perspective on this. He was a retired police detective. I leaned toward him with my elbows on the table. "Harry, what's your take on this? Inside job?"

He sipped his coffee before answering. "Well, it seems to me, that's the only conclusion to make. I spoke with the officer who came day before yesterday, and he said they were investigating, but I'm not at liberty to divulge any information he gave me."

Bessie crossed her arms over her ample bosom. "Humph, nobody better try to take any of my things. I'll clobber them with my baseball bat."

I swallowed a chuckle at that. Everyone knew Bessie slept with her "weapon" beside her bed ever since the gardener had been found dead in my flower bed last fall.

Doris Barton wrinkled her nose and pushed a fork through her omelet. "Well, I hope Ellie doesn't call that grandson of hers. He complains about everything. He'd have a heyday with this one."

Ellie's grandson loved her and got involved with everything going on in the Ellie's building. I considered him to be an arrogant young man with more money than common sense.

The idea of stealing going on in Spring Hills bothered me, and I was anxious to get alone with

Ben and Harry to hash out a few theories. This would be even a lot easier and less dangerous than our work with Pete's murder. One thing about Ben, he loved solving mysteries as much as I did.

Ben I may be good friends, but he'd indicated more than once he'd like it to be more. I did enjoy his company, and we had some good times together, but that's as far as I wanted to go right now. Since my Jack's death five years ago, I haven't really been interested in another relationship. Ben and I also had unfinished business concerning his relationship to the Lord.

I glanced to my right where he was sitting. He didn't seem to be listening with his full attention. Probably trying to figure out the same things I've been thinking.

Soon as we finished breakfast, I'd get him and Harry to come to my cottage and discuss the possibilities of the case. Even with the police involved, we could still do more good. Many, if not most of the residents were reluctant to talk with the police after Pete's death.

With my good intuition and love for sleuthing, and their crime expertise, we could solve this in no time. Ben's investigative days as a defense lawyer gave him the know how to work on the thefts.

Bessie cooed and flashed her dimples. "Oh, Ben, don't forget the spring bridge tournament is coming up, and we're having a session this afternoon."

Ben shrugged. "I just don't have the time."

With her curls and dimples, Bessie must have looked just like Shirley Temple in her childhood. I hoped he meant he'd be spending that time with me and Harry.

Doris pushed back her chair. "If you'll excuse me, I'm going to change for my water aerobics class."

Doris is quiet and doesn't always participate in our conversations, but she's faithful to whatever she gets involved in, and she loved swimming.

When I rose to leave, Ben followed me to the foyer. "Abby, mind if we talk a little?"

I smiled and shook my head. "I know just what you want. We're going to investigate these thefts aren't we?"

"Ah, yes. With four thefts now, it's time to take action. Let's go down to your place. We'll have more privacy there."

He held the door open then accompanied me down the path. At least i had mercy on him this time and strolled beside him instead of loping ahead as I usually did.

I keep in shape on the golf course a few afternoons a week, and I walked as much as I could. Poor Ben always had a hard time keeping up with me, but today I cut him slack.

Ben pointed over to where the ground crew edged and mowed. "They've done a good job with Pete gone. The flowers are as beautiful as ever."

Our grounds were full of spring blossoms, and the early morning chill gave way to the sunshine. "These are perfect days for golf."

Ben shrugged his shoulders. "I still don't see any point to a game where all you do is hit a ball, chase it, and then hit it again to get it into a little hole."

"I know. You've told me enough times what a waste of time it is, but I enjoy it."

He had no response for that. When we arrived at my cottage, I sank into one of the plastic chairs on my porch and nodded for him to join me.

Ben eased down and relaxed. "You want to go first?"

"Yes. I have a million questions and observations. First off, this has to be an inside theft. Think about it, Ben, no one can get into this place after seven p.m. without a pass or being let in by the attendant. And they have to sign in too."

"That's obvious, but who do you suspect? Employee or resident?" Ben smoothed back his thick, white hair, ruffled by the slight breeze.

"Well, I'm a bit puzzled. However, let's look at it this way. Ellie is in room one thirty-five on the first floor. The other three thefts occurred in close proximity."

Ben scratched his chin. "And how do you know that?"

"I go over and read to Ellie three times a week. You were right about her eyesight."

He chuckled. "I know, but it wasn't a nice thing to say. I apologize." His elbows rested on the chair arms, and he made a peak with his fingers. "You say the other ladies live close to Ellie?"

"All are on the same wing, so it could be someone attending to those rooms. Of course that gives us a good list of suspects." I jumped up. "Let me get a pad and pen to write all this down."

Ben stopped me. "Do you have any fully-leaded coffee? That decaf they serve here doesn't help my thinker."

"Sure. Be back in a jiffy."

I poured two cups from the coffee pot I kept on for this very purpose. I returned with two mugs of steaming coffee and set them on the table between the chairs. Then I retrieved the pad and pen I had stashed in my pants pocket.

He wrapped his hands around the warmth and savored the aroma rising from the mug. His eyebrows knit together. "Who takes care of the ladies in those rooms?" He downed a swig of his coffee.

"I'm not sure, but I can find out from Ellie." I began writing on the pad. "If I'm not mistaken, the exit is open during the day from the inside only and you need a passkey to get in from the outside."

"Right, and it's locked in both directions at night. Shall we begin with the staff?"

He grinned and waited for my response, which would be yes. "Exactly what I hoped you'd say. Now let's see what we have."

"What we need are those new brochures with the floor plans. That way we can see who might have access."

"That's easy to get. The office if full of them since Noreen had them printed last fall."

"Then all we need to do is to come up a list of all employees." I tapped my lips with the end of my pen, resisting the urge the chew on it like I usually did when I pondered unanswered questions.

"Are you going to wait until your usual time to go see Ellie?"

"Yes. I see no need to change our routine. We can talk about her pearls then."

Ben rubbed his hands together. "Sounds like a plan to me. Say we meet back here about half an hour before dinner and see what we have."

I leaned back in her chair. "Sounds good to me, but it sure would be nice if I find the pearls for Ellie while I'm there."

"Yes, that would be nice, but I have the feeling that isn't going to happen."

Ben left, but I remained on the porch. This little case, as I'd already begun to think of it, might take more time than we thought. But what did that matter. As I've said more than once, all we had around here was time. A bark from inside the house brought me to my feet.

Poor Mitzi. I'd completely forgotten she was still closed up in her carrier. Thinking about lost jewelry would have to wait.

Social Media:
Facebook: Martha L. Rogers
Twitter: @MarthaRogers2
Website: www.marthawrogers.com

Pinterest: www.pinterest.com/grammymartha/

Love in the Bayou City of Texas:
Love on Trial
Forgiving Love

River Walk Christmas
Best Laid Plans
Not on the Menu

Series:

Winds Across the Prairie:	***The Homeward***
Journey	
Becoming Lucy	*Love Stays True*
Morning for Dove	*Love Finds*
Faith	
Finding Becky	*Love Never*
Fails	
Caroline's Choice	
Amelia's Journey	
Christmas at Holly Hill	
Seasons of the Heart	
Summer Dream	
Autumn Song	
Winter Promise	
Spring Hope	

Made in the USA
Lexington, KY
03 November 2019

56520455R00119